BROOKLYN
WASHINGTON

A HOT ROD NOVELLA
by s r puvogel

Dedication

This book is dedicated to my son Steven and his
family for project
"Keep Grandpa Alive"
I cannot possibly thank him enough for his help
with my battle with leukemia

BROOKLYN WASHINGTON   A HOT ROD
NOVELLA
(Revised Edition)
Copyright 2023
s r puvogel

TABLE OF CONTENTS

CHAPTER ONE

"Cars and Characters"

"I'm 50 years old, you'd think this stuff wouldn't bother me, but now that the car show is happening this weekend, Marty's disappearance really hit me hard." Ray said.

"I know you've had a tough year, with your friend Marty disappearing, and now you're going to the "Rod Run" car show without him for the first time in a long time. I'm sorry you're going through this," Ray's mom Martha said.

Ray was happy that his mother was there for him. His father unfortunately passed away in 2015. Ray was named after his father. His dad was known as "Big Ray", and he was called "Ray Ray", a name his mother gave him when he was little.

"Now Ray Ray, take care of yourself, I don't want you to disappear too." Martha grabbed Ray's hands to get his attention, and looked into his eyes, " I want you to have fun, but I don't have a good feeling about this weekend." This shook Ray to his core, his mom often had premonitions that would come true.

"Mom, I've put a new battery in the Ford, so I don't anticipate any vehicle problems. This should be a fun weekend, and with any luck someone will have knowledge about what happened to Marty. I just hope what I find out isn't bad news." said Ray.

Ray gave his mom a kiss on the top of her head and said "I love you, and thank you for letting me take Dad's car. If nothing else, I can relive some of the good old days in it. Don't worry about me, mom. I know this will be another fun adventure."

"Also, thank you for watching "Molly" again this weekend." Ray said. "Molly" is Ray's Lhasa Apso, or maybe it's the other way around and Ray is "Molly's" human. "Molly" knew how to pull at Ray's heart strings, she had him wrapped around her little paws.

Ray picked up "Molly" and gave her a hug, "Molly" looked up at Ray and gave him the guilts like "You're not leaving me with grandma again, are you?"

"She is no problem, she is my granddogger, after all," Martha said. "She spent most of last year with me while you were on the road. Besides, you may not get her back from me after you get home from this weekend, she is so adorable!" Ray hated to leave "Molly" with his mom again, but dogs were not allowed at the car show.

Ray and Marty had traditionally driven their vintage cars to the "Rod Run" car show every year, except last year when Ray was on a tour of the United States and Canada with his kustom car "Invictus". Ray is well known as a kustom car builder. The term kustom with a "k" and not a "c" came about to refer to exclusively American cars originally built between the late 1930's through the early 1960's that are highly modified. It's not just contemporary car stylizing.

His car "Invictus" is a highly kustomized 1959 Buick Invicta convertible. Ray is a firm believer in traditional kustoms. "Invictus" was lowered, had Chrome "Lakes" exhaust pipes on the side, wide white wall tires, "Smoothie" chrome wheels with "baby moon" center caps for that vintage wheel look.

The interior has white tuck and roll upholstery on swivel bucket seats. A vintage kustom has to have a TV set installed in it. So a center console was installed with a vintage black and white picture tube because a modern screen would not look right in it. Any place that would have been carpeted was covered with fuzzy "angel hair" upholstery material. This reflects the old kustomizer saying "If it don't go, upholster it." In other words, if it's not part of the drivetrain-upholster it! Oh yeah, it's painted metal flake Orange. "Invictus" had won many awards and kept Ray on the road for most of the year.

Ray was very fond of the '59 Buick, it had those "canted" headlights where the inner ones were lower in the grill than the outer ones. In addition, the fenders formed sort of a hood over the headlights which gave the '59 Buick an evil look to it. A great starting point for any car kustomizer. But this weekend Ray would be driving his dad's car, a 1950 Ford "Shoebox".

A "shoebox" is a car with styling that has flat sides, unlike pre-war cars that had fenders that protruded from the body. Ford initially introduced the "shoebox" styling in 1949 and carried the same body over to the 1950 model. The name "shoebox" comes from the fact that it looks like a shoe box. Ford still retained the venerable flathead that they first released in the 1932 Ford. The flathead motor became a hotrodders favorite over all those years, so speed equipment was easy to come by for that motor. Big Ray's car was lowered, had a chopped top, and was heavily modified with speed equipment. Big Ray did all this after high school graduation, before he joined the Air Force.

It had a "3/4 race" camshaft, which meant more power than stock, but not full "racing" power. It was about as radical a camshaft as you would want for a car you drive on the street. It wasn't a brand name camshaft, but a "regrind" with specific lobe profiles made for his dad. The motor or "mill" as they were called was topped with an Edelbrock multiple carburetor intake manifold setup with Stromberg 97 carburetors.

The exhaust was handled with special exhaust headers that Ray's dad had built. The headers routed the exhaust through Chrome "Lakes" pipes. The term "Lakes" pipes came about because the hot rodders that raced on the dry lake beds of Southern California used them. But more than that, they were a cheap and easy way to route the exhaust away from the car. It doesn't get much simpler than a length of pipe that runs the length of the rocker panel, sweeping out in front of the rear wheels. The Ford was a two-door "club coupe" body style.

The wheels are the factory ones painted black and they had what's called "Full Moon" wheel covers. This was simply a spun aluminum disc that covered the entire wheel except a small portion around the outside rim (where you could see the wheel color). And of course, the tires were wide white walls.

The Ford was originally painted black, and that fit in perfectly with the hot rod image.

But for Christmas in 1992, Ray told his dad he would paint the car any color he wanted. Ford had just come out with Cayman Green Metallic on the 1992 Thunderbird. This was the color his dad was absolutely in love with. Not a traditional hot rod color at all, but that's what Dad wanted, so that's what he got.

The car also has the ultra rare aftermarket MESCO "swinging eye" center fog light. It replaced the chrome "bullet" in the center of the grill with a light that would turn whatever direction you moved the steering wheel. Just like on the 1948 Tucker. It had a complicated linkage setup that was connected to the factory tie rods. When Ray was a kid, he used to play in the garage turning the steering wheel back and forth just to see the light shine in different directions. Ray loved this car, and he was lucky enough that his dad let him drive it during his high school years.

Big Ray had found a pair of license plates at a local old car swap meet from Benton County Washington (the county with "R" plates) that read

"Ray 050", so he bought those and they were were re-licensed to the car in 1970. They are 1954 plates, but big Ray figured he would never find a plate with such perfect numbers on them, so he used them. Besides, he liked the green color.

When Ray's father was in the Air Force he was stationed at McChord Air Force Base near Tacoma Washington. He fell in love with the Pacific Northwest during the time he was there.. When Big Ray got out of the Air Force he took a job at the big kite factory (AKA Boeing).

Ray's parents moved to the Seattle "bedroom" community of Federal Way Washington in the early 60's, from the upper peninsula of Michigan. People from the upper peninsula of Michigan are known as "Yoopers," and like a lot of "Yoopers," both of his parents were of Finnish descent.

The Finnish-American accent consists of words spoken with deliberate choice, rolled "R's", and every single letter of the word pronounced. Ray loved his parents and loved listening to the way they spoke. It brought comfort to him

When Ray was a little boy, he could always tell when his dad was coming home from work because the flathead motor would cause static on the TV set. This was back in the days before cable TV, when you still had a TV antenna on the roof. It was a wonderful and idyllic family life filled with love. Ray terribly missed his dad, and secretly wished to hear that Ford flathead television static again.

Ray's best friend, Martin "Marty" Miles also loved Big Ray's car. He loved it so much that he had Ray build an exact duplicate of it.

The one exception is Marty's club coupe is black in color as Big Ray's originally was.

Ray and Marty had been friends since grade school, when they were in Boy Scouts together. And in high school they would cruise old Highway 99 in Big Ray's Ford.

Marty had developed computer software that made him a very rich man. In fact, he was a billionaire. That never stopped him from enjoying old cars though. The '50 Ford clone he had Ray build would only come out once a year and that was for the "Rod Run to the End of the World" car show at Long Beach Washington. Marty liked having a car that no one knew was his. It brought back high school memories of cruising in a black 1950 Ford.

Marty and Ray would take the clone '50 Ford, and whatever secret project Ray was working on, to "Rod Run", as everyone in Washington state called it. They would go to the car show incognito, so they could be left alone. Marty, because he was rich, and Ray, because he wanted to enjoy a car show without having to talk about business. They wore long straight hair wigs that made them look like 1970s rock and rollers. Marty went by the name "Jim", and Ray went by the name "Mike". They had been doing this for so long they looked like a couple of old hippies now.

Marty went to the "Rod Run" car show last year by himself because Ray was on tour with Invictus. Marty was never seen again after the car show events. Ray checked with the regulars he had seen every year at the show if they had seen "Jim", and the answer was "yes". People saw him there, and at the after cruise that night.

Ray was beating himself up with worry that he may have missed some safety item when he built Marty's car, and that's what happened. If he only had gone to the car show with Marty, there's a good chance Marty would still be around today.

Ray was taking his dad's car for two reasons. One was that he had no secret project cars this year and no one knew about Big Ray's car, so he could have some anonymity. And two, maybe someone would see the car and know something about what happened to Marty last year. After all, there aren't that many cars out there with that center fog light.

Ray still had a gut feeling that something he did may have caused Marty's disappearance. He had no clue what it possibly could be though. Perhaps the doubts in Ray's mind were caused by the FBI showing up in his shop monthly. Marty's software business included government contracts that were sensitive in nature. A disappearance by a rich man, let alone one involved in high security government contracts is enough to raise a lot of red flags. Terrorists, or at least foreign agents were not ruled out of the equation.

CHAPTER TWO

"One for the Road"

Ray checked his vintage Rolex and knew it was time to grab the last two things he needed before he hit the road, his long hair wig and a beat up old Seahawks baseball cap. His disguise did not fool everyone but fooled enough people that he could enjoy the car show.

Ray put the key in the ignition, turned it, and the Ford fired to life. He put the wig and the old Seahawks cap on and headed for Interstate 5 southbound. It is about a 3-hour drive to the Long Beach peninsula on the southwest corner of Washington State.

The "Beach Barons" car club put on the "Rod Run to the End of the World" car show the second weekend of September every year. The "Beach Barons" had put on the show for many years at their top-notch facility on the North End of the Long Beach peninsula and were a well-respected car club in Washington State.

It is said that Washington state has two seasons, August, and the rest of the year. The good weather in August almost always goes into September. Perfect car show weather. The car show normally had 800 to 900 cars in it, and was traditionally the last car show of the season. It drew people from both the Seattle and the Portland Oregon area.

The show was both days of the weekend, with a cruise after Saturday's show. The cruise would often run till 2:00 in the morning. A lot of people would show up just to take part in the cruise. It was like a Mardi Gras for cars. Spectators would set up their lawn chairs on both sides of the road. The old car faithful cheered on the cruisers for the entire 26 miles of the Long Beach peninsula. It was truly the Church of the Cruise.

People would bring out garden hoses and water down the road encouraging people to do burnouts. Of course, the police were there in force to discourage people from doing burnouts. It was a huge party that celebrated the automobile.

This is the reason that Ray and Marty would go there every year.

There are chain hotels on the Long Beach peninsula, but Ray and Marty would always stay at one of those little "Beach" motels. The people were friendly, and there was always a clam cleaning sink outside if you were clam digging while you were there. But "Rod Run" weekend is about cars, and not a weekend for digging clams. The rooms always had a faint smell of wet sand, and that seemed to make them special. Ray had his reservations at his favorite Beach motel and was looking forward to getting there to watch the cars arriving and cruising around Friday night.

It was a typical Friday afternoon and traffic was bumper to bumper on Interstate 5. The second that Ray turned off Interstate 5 he could feel his blood pressure lower, he knew it would be State highways and country roads the rest of the way to the beach.

The country roads joined Highway 101 at Aberdeen Washington. About 10 miles south of Aberdeen is a wayside called Artic. There is a tavern and an RV park there. Just beyond the wayside of Artic is a sign on the left side of the road that directs you to the communities of Vesta and Brooklyn. Ray glanced over and thought to himself "One of these days I'm going to check out Brooklyn."

Ray had never heard of Vesta, but he had heard of Brooklyn. He knew that off-road rally races were held there every year, and that it had a tavern. Just having a tavern there was a good enough reason to stop. But not today, he wanted to make it to the beach before 5:00.

The thought had occurred to him that he would come back and watch one of the rally races that are held there. The eastbound road out of Brooklyn is a 20 mile stretch of gravel road ideal for rally racing. He also had an open invitation from one of his kustom car customers to join her rally team on one of the events. Maybe next year.

Brooklyn itself is not a city or town, more of a community. It has the tavern and the North River School district as its two main buildings. At one point it was a vibrant little town, but that had all gone away. Vesta is now just a few houses alongside North River Road.

When Ray made it to the Long Beach peninsula he glanced at the Rolex and saw it was 4:00, that meant he still had time to stop in Ilwaco, and join the slow drags. The slow drags were not part of the car show, but they were traditionally held the day before the show.

Slow drags are a competition between two cars to see who can bump the throttle once, and coast as close as possible to a designated finish line. Which was usually just a fire hose stretched across the street. There are no prizes or awards, it's just bragging rights for a silly little contest.

Ray figured that the slow drags would be a great way for people to take notice of the Ford. The spectators and contestants at the Friday night slow drags would be at the car show on Saturday. Turning the steering wheel quickly left and right is a good way to slow down the car if you've given it too much gas. It would also bring attention to the center fog light that swiveled.

There are no vehicle age requirements for the cars or trucks in the slow drags, so you could be "racing" against a modern car or truck. There aren't any dress or safety codes either. Ray got in line for his first race and next to him was a late sixties Cadillac convertible with 6 very tipsy ladies in sundresses and floppy hats standing up in the car. No one was even going to look at his car at this rate. Ray did his best to attract as much attention to his car as possible, but the ladies were the center of attention. And what's worse is that they won and eliminated Ray from the race. This is a very light-hearted event, and all is fair.

Ray had figured it was no sense to hang around, so he just headed back for his motel to watch people cruise.

When Ray got to the motel and checked in, he asked the motel owners if they remember if "Jim" had been there last year and they said "Yes." He then asked if he seemed stressed out or anything unusual was going on with him, and the answer was "No." Bud the motel owner said "I remember him saying what a good time he had. He made reservations for this year's show. Do you know what time "Jim" is going to be here tonight?" Ray answered back "No. No, I don't know what time he will be here. I hope he makes it here pretty soon." Ray was pretty sure "Jim" was not going to be there at all.

He parked the Ford out front of the motel, facing the street and grabbed a lawn chair out of the trunk, and set it up next to the car. It was now time for a cup of coffee and to sit and watch people driving their hot rods and vintage cars into town. After all, tomorrow is going to be a long day at the car show.

Amongst the endless parade of hot rods and vintage cars driving into town, Ray recognized a couple cars that he built. He hoped he would not run into those people tomorrow.

Ray got up early the next morning, made a pot of coffee, filled his thermos and hit the road to the car show.

Ray got to the car show around 8:00 a.m., he picked up his goodie bag of stuff that is always given out to car show participants. He found his parking spot and got ready for the day. Ray was pleased with his assigned spot. He was between a 1939 Ford Deluxe Coupe and a 1956 Ford Customline Tudor Sedan. It made a great illustration on how Ford body styles had changed over those years with those three cars in a row Ray had a '39 Ford Coupe in the shop right now that he was customizing. It's always good to look at someone else's ideas for what you are building. You never want to copy it but take cues from what they have done.

Ray got out his lawn chairs and his pop-up canopy for protection from the sun. You always bring more chairs than you need because one of the fun parts of a car show is talking with other people. He set up the pop-up canopy behind his car so people could take pictures of the car, and it would not be in the way.

Now that everything was set up, it was time for a cup of coffee, and to check what is in this year's goodie bag. He gave a quick look at next year's car show brochures. In addition to the car show brochures, a car detailing product, a baseball cap, and a dash plaque, were in the goodie bag.

Ray introduced himself to his car show neighbors. An older couple owned the 39 Ford Deluxe, and a younger couple had the two door 56 Ford Customline. People at the "Rod Run" car show are always friendly. Everybody agreed to watch each other's cars when someone needed to take a potty break, or just walk around the car show.

Ray was in full "Mike" mode, he wanted to enjoy the car show and not answer questions about what was in his shop. He did ask his car show neighbors if they knew anything about "Jim". They said they vaguely remember the car last year, because it also had that center fog light, but they didn't remember the guy that was driving it. A lot of people will just park their car at a car show and go wandering about looking at other cars, and that is undoubtedly what Marty did last year. This may be tougher than he thought trying to find a lead about Marty.

The older couple took off walking around the car show leaving Ray to watch their car. He heard some people talking about it and that they had said "That is a beautiful 1940 Ford." That immediately triggered the inner "car geek" in Ray. He got out of his chair walked up to the people and said "It's tough to tell the '39 from the '40 Ford, but the difference is 1939 Ford closed cars (not a convertible) have the windshield wipers mounted above the windshield and 1940 Fords have the windshield wipers mounted below the windshield. This is a '39." He also said that he was currently building a 1939 Ford and that they had good taste to recognize that this car was beautiful. He also pointed out some of the special features the '39 Deluxe had over the '39 Standard models. As he was speaking, he realized that he was jeopardizing his incognito disguise as "Mike".

As if almost on cue he hears a female voice say to him "Ray Ray?" To which Ray responded "No, my name is Mike." Ray then turned around and saw that it was Mary, the gal with the rally car, and a red and white 1956 Chevy Nomad he built for her. He thought he had seen the Nomad cruising around town last night, but he just wasn't sure. He knew for sure now. Mary is in her early 40s, a tall, trim, and gorgeous lady with lots of money, and the money looked good on her. Mary was very private about her source of income, but she paid her bill when the car was built, and that was the important thing. Getting paid on time was always a plus in Ray's book.

Mary's blonde hair was in a ponytail, and she was wearing car show chic, tight blue jeans and the car show t-shirt tied in a knot at the bottom. It was tough for Ray to take his eyes off of her.

Mary had a zest for life, owning the nicest cars, and spending time behind the wheel racing some of them

Ray had spent too much time going over the details of the Nomad with her, when he built it, to deny who he was. But he figured he would try and deny it one more time. It didn't work. She said "If you're not Ray Ray of Ray Ray Kustoms, why does the license plate say 'Ray' on it?" To which Ray replied, "This is my dad's car." Which is true, but not an admission that he's not Ray Ray.

Ray realized that he better come clean and admit who he is, there's a good chance she will spend more money at his shop.

Ray motioned to Mary to step over by the Ford, and then admitted "You got me, I like coming to this car show incognito so I can enjoy it and not talk about business." "I see you brought the Nomad down here, how has it been treating you?" Ray inquired.

Mary answered back "It is a dream to drive. I have been thinking about you, and wondering if you would work on some of my other cars?"

Ray responded, "I'm trying to keep my business strictly vintage and traditional hot rod vehicles only."

"Money is not an issue for me," she said. "I just want the best driving and handling vehicles that I can possibly get."

Ray then said "I will think about it, but absolutely no promises." He then noticed some kids about ready to stick their hands on the '39 Ford and said "I have to watch this car, I promised the owners that I would" "Touch base with me sometime next week, and we will discuss it."

Abruptly shouting "Hey you kids, don't touch that car!" was a good way to end the conversation with Mary.

Ray had managed to stay a bachelor all of his life, he loved cars and dogs too. That was more than enough for him. He certainly did not want to end up in a relationship where he was just some rich gal's mechanic. He did not need her money at all.

He was in the process of selling Invictus for an "undisclosed six-figure sum." Ray had built lots of cars that he sold for "undisclosed six figure amounts". He was not as rich as Marty, but he could retire right now and live off the money he made from all the cars he sold. It would be nice to retire, do some traveling with his dog "Molly", and leave the daily grind behind.

The sun came out and it was starting to get hot, so Ray went back to the shade of his pop-up canopy and sat down.

He grabbed a sandwich out of the cooler, poured another cup of coffee, and waited for the older folks to get back, so he could walk around the car show. The couple with the 56 Ford had been walking around the show all morning. He was hoping that someone would come back soon cuz he had been drinking a lot of coffee and really needed to use the restroom.

He was keeping his eyes on both cars when he heard someone say "Gee that's a nice 55 Ford." The inner car geek in him struck again and he leapt out of the chair like someone poked him with a pin. But this time he stayed under the shade of the canopy and said to the people "That's a '56, it has the elliptical shaped Park lamps, a '55 has round Park lamps". They looked at him, and then they looked at his car. They noticed the center fog light and asked Ray a question.

"Were you here last year? I think you were behind us on the road on the way back to Seattle. I could see a car in the mirror following me with a center fog light that moved left and right. I thought it may have been a Tucker at first, but I didn't recall seeing a Tucker at the car show. You were quite a ways behind me until you turned off before Highway 107."

Ray almost choked on his sandwich. These people had seen Marty on Sunday on the road home. At least they had seen Marty's car.

"No, that wasn't me, I have a friend that has a car just like this but painted black. Where did you say he turned off at?"

"I think it was at the road that had the sign about Vesta and Brooklyn" the guy said. "One of these days I'm going to check out Brooklyn." he added.

Was this the clue that Ray was hoping to find? He certainly hoped so.

The older couple showed up at their car and Ray made a bee-line for the restroom. He then went back to the car and chatted with the older couple about the cars that were there. Especially a '56 Nomad that he initially wanted to avoid, but now she may have some information about Brooklyn because she rally raced there.

Ultimately, he decided today was not the day to talk to her, he just wanted to enjoy the car show.

Ray had a relaxing afternoon because he knew that tomorrow he was going to check out Brooklyn. If nothing else he was going to have a beer at the Brooklyn tavern.

It was like a burden had been lifted, at last he had a clue to where Marty may be.

Ray spent the evening cruising up and down the Long Beach peninsula with all the other cars, totally enjoying himself.

CHAPTER THREE

"I'm going to check out Brooklyn"

Ray got up early Sunday morning. He had absolutely no thought about heading back for the second day of the car show, he was going to check out Brooklyn.

All the luggage was packed into the car and Ray headed to the office to check out and make next year's reservations.

Ray opened the door to the motel office and "Reverb", the owner's collie, went up to greet him. "Reverb" is a very friendly dog, always looking to be petted, and Ray was glad to oblige him. This was one of the reasons that Ray chose this motel every year is that the owners, Bud and Marilyn were dog owners. And the motel was dog friendly, he would bring "Molly" here at least once a year, unfortunately still incognito as "Mike".

"If "Reverb" is bothering you, you can just tell him to "go lay down"" said Marilyn "No he isn't, I enjoy seeing him, he is always so happy" Ray responded. And then Ray added ""Jim" loves "Reverb" too, did he show up this weekend? I didn't see him at all." Ray knew what the answer would be, but it never hurt to ask.

"No, he never showed up," Marilyn said. "We ended up renting that room to someone else late Friday night. Unfortunately, "Jim" has lost his spot for the room. Those people checked out real early this morning and paid for the room for next year."

"Mike," did you want to make reservations for next year?"

"Yes I do, I'm looking forward to seeing you folks again, let me pay for next year. I sure hope "Jim" can make it, maybe he and I can double up in one room," Ray said. Paying for next year's room was the best way to save it. Rooms were always booked a year ahead of time.

Ray paid for next year's room, thanked Marilyn and grabbed a cup of coffee and a couple cinnamon rolls for the road from the complimentary breakfast. One last stop for gas, then it's off to Brooklyn!

Most of the stations on the peninsula were out of premium gas due to all the hot rods being in town. Ray found one that still had some and pulled up to the pump and went inside to pay.

When he came back outside, there was Mary and her Nomad. He figured it was a good time to talk with her because he could take off as soon as he filled his tank.

"Hey ya, Ray Ray!" She exclaimed. "Hey ya!" Ray answered back. "I have a question for you, it's about the town of Brooklyn." Ray said. "I am thinking about heading there this morning."

"It's not really a town, more of a community, it has a tavern and a school building." Mary answered back.

"I'm going to be doing some 'pre-running' there with my WRX Rally car (Subaru WRX) next weekend to familiarize myself with the rally course for the race coming up in a month. Why don't you join me?" Mary said.

"I just might do that," Ray said. "I have a friend that went that direction, and he just disappeared."

"We can hang out at the tavern, and they are closing down the gravel road next Sunday morning and you can watch me practice my 'ditch hooking'" Mary said.

"Practice your what?" Ray quizzed.

"Ditch hooking." Mary immediately replied "In rally driving, to prevent losing momentum on a corner, you drop your inside front wheel into the ditch, floor it, and power around the corner."

"Oh, ok, that makes sense," Ray replied. "Sounds like fun."

"We can ask around at the tavern if anyone knows what happened to your friend, " Mary said. " I would head there today with you except I inherited several properties in Grays Harbor, and I have to get ready for my annual inspection of them this week."

"You could come down there early next weekend. I have a big house in Aberdeen you would be welcome to stay there." said Mary with a sly smile on her face.

"I might just do that, I would have to bring "Molly" with me though," Ray said.

"Who's "Molly"?" Mary said as the smile went out of her face.

"She's my Lhasa Apso puppy dog, I have been leaving her with my mom far too many times, she needs to spend a weekend with me." Ray said.

The smile came back to Mary, she said "I have a Lhasa Apso too, her name is "Kissa". I think they could have a great time together!"

Upon hearing that, Ray broke out into laughter. "Did you know kissa is the Finnish word for cat?" He said.

"That I didn't know, I named her that because she was always giving me puppy dog kisses." Mary answered back while laughing.

This was turning into a date with Mary, and that was something Ray wasn't ready to do.

"I can't make a sure promise that I will be there next weekend, I'm finishing up the sale of Invictus, the car I took on tour last year." Ray said.

"Maybe I can come down here the Sunday of the race though." He added.

Mary scribbled her phone number on a piece of paper and handed it to Ray. "Please give me a call if you're going to come down, I'll make sure I have a room ready for you and "Molly"."

Just then the pump clicked off, and Ray said "It was good to see you again, I will get in touch with you if I can wrap up the business with Invictus".

Ray and Mary exchanged "goodbye and safe travels" with each other, and Ray got into the Ford.

Ray looked into the rear-view mirror, checked the wig, and the Seahawks Cap, it's finally time for Brooklyn.

That conversation with Mary cleared up one of the questions he had about her, where her money came from. The other question he couldn't figure out is why someone that was maybe 10 years younger than him, was interested in him.

After a busy weekend, Ray just wanted to listen to some rock and roll. The old Ford still had the original AM radio, so Ray turned it on hoping to find a radio station. He found a clear signal station out of Astoria Oregon that was running a syndicated oldies program.

This would be ideal driving music Ray figured, as this music probably played when the car was new. The program had one of those announcers that gave a bibliography of the song he was about to play. It was interesting to find out about all of those old artists.

After about an hour of driving, Ray made it to the right-hand turn to Vesta and Brooklyn. He checked his Rolex. It was only 10:00 a.m.

He knew Washington state law wouldn't let the tavern open till noon, so he figured he had some time to drive around.

It was a beautiful sunny morning and the fragrant smell of the trees made it a pleasant drive.

The radio announcer said that the next song was arguably the very first rock and roll song, and it had to do with a car. He then announced that it was Jackie Brenston and his Delta Cats, with "Rocket 88."

Ray reached down and turned up the radio, he liked the idea of an old song about a car.

The piano intro was playing as Ray noticed the sign for a narrow bridge ahead. He could see that the morning sun was causing fog/steam to rise from the river below.

As Ray drove on to the bridge, he was surrounded by the steam coming off the river. He slowed to an almost complete stop as Jackie was singing- "Goin' 'round the corner and get a beer, Everybody in my car is gonna to take a little trip, Move on out, oozin' and a cruisin' along."

And then the Ford went...

"BAWHOOM!"

The engine died and the car coasted to the end of the bridge and onto the road.

It took Ray a moment to regain his composure. He turned the ignition switch off and back on and the car started right up like nothing happened.

He could tell the radio was still on, but the station was gone. Ray turned the dial and eventually found a station that was playing Eddie Fisher. That was not Ray's kind of music, so he turned off the radio.

Always looking for old cars, Ray spotted a very clean '55 Chevy 150 four-door sedan parked in a driveway and thought to himself he may come back and make an offer for that car. It was the most base model four-door Chevy offered, but '55's are getting hard to come by, and it would make a great project car. It was definitely a local car because it had a green 1955 "H" license plate which was correct for Grays Harbor County.

Ray noticed the names on the mailboxes, a lot of them ended in "-inen" or "-ala", which meant he was in a Finnish community. He knew that the town of Naselle was predominantly Finnish because he had relatives there. He was not aware of any other communities.

Ray looked forward to stopping and talking to locals to hear that Finnish-American accent and maybe find out information about Marty.

He also noticed that the newspaper receptacles on the mailboxes were cylindrical metal tubes. Like they were in the old days. Not like the plastic rectangular ones you see now. The strange thing was that they all looked new with fresh "Aberdeen Daily World" printing on them. Aberdeen is a close local town that had a population of around 5,000 people.

The strangeness continued; a 1947 Dodge Custom came down on the road towards him with green 1955 license plates. It was just regular "H" license plates, no unique numbers on it at all. If it was running original plates, they would have been white in color with green letters.

Ray just figured it was an old car collector, so he waved to the guy, and he waved back.

Ray noticed a red and white sign that was attached to a fence post, and it said "Ladies!", And then in 100 ft one that said, "Does your husband," then after another 100 ft. one that said, "Grunt and Grumble" Then, "Rant and Rave?" And then, "Shoot the Brute Some"....

CHAPTER FOUR

"Burma-Shave"

"Burma-Shave!" the last sign said.

Ray got a big laugh out of that. Big Ray had told him about Burma-Shave signs, but he had never seen any.

Obviously, someone had made some reproduction signs and posted them here. What a neat touch on this country road, he thought.

Ray was beginning to think that he was in Cuba or some other third world country because he didn't see any vehicles newer than about mid-50s. And they all had the 1954/1955 green license plates.

Ray came across three Ford model T's, parked in front of a farm house with one of them, a Fordor sedan having a "for sale" sign in the back window. The other two were coupe models.

Also parked out front of the same house was a "doodlebug" tractor made from a model T. During World War II, tractors were in short supply. Companies like "Mak-a-Tractor" made conversion kits to convert the model T into a tractor. For $199 you could get a kit that had two large diameter steel wheels with metal cleats on them that replaced the stock rear wheels. It also had a power takeoff conversion for the rear axle to power farm equipment. Everything from the windshield forward was retained, and the rest of the body was removed, while a single person seat was mounted in front of the steering wheel.

Ray wanted to see if he could buy the two model T coupes and the tractor conversion too.

This was undoubtedly the place he was going to spend time at until the tavern opened.

The Fordor sedan had a price of $400 on it. It was in immaculate shape, the upholstery looked like it had never been sat on. Ray couldn't get the money out of his wallet fast enough, he wanted that car.

Ray walked up to the farmhouse and knocked on the door. The man that answered the door looked like he was in his 80's or 90's. He spoke and said "Can I help you, chief?"

Ray immediately recognized the Finnish-American accent, but was taken aback by the chief comment.

"Chief?" Ray asked.

The old man said "You're an Indian aren't you? You have a totem pole on your hat."

It took Ray a moment to realize that he was talking about his Seattle Seahawks baseball cap. He then said "This is the logo for the Seattle Seahawks football team."

"Never heard of 'em, are they on television? " The old man asked.

"Yes they are, every Sunday during football season," Ray answered.

"Don't know about that, don't have a television. You can't get it down here in the valley." the old man said.

Ray then realized he still had his wig on and probably looked native American. He said "I'll be right back." He went to the car and threw the wig and the baseball cap under the seat.

Ray had to think of something quick, he said "I was at a costume party and I forgot to take off the wig." The old guy didn't question why Ray was at a costume party on Sunday morning, so Ray just let it slide.

He then said to the old man, realizing he was Finnish "My name is Reino Raittinen (his actual name, pronounced 'Ray-no Rite-tin-en') and I would like to buy that model T Fordor."

"It looks like it's in pretty good shape, and it's well worth the $400" Ray said. "I am fine with the price."

"Are the coupes for sale too?" Ray inquired.

The old man spoke with a deliberate cadence, and chose his words "It's great to meet you Reino, my name is Uno (pronounced Ooh-no). And yes, that one is in pretty good shape, the coupes are not for sale though."

"How about the tractor, is that for sale?" Ray inquired.

"No, I need that to work around the farm." Uno responded.

"Let me know if you change your mind, I would love to buy them from you." Ray said.

Uno then spoke up and said, "I have some parts cars, if you're interested."

"How many?" Ray asked.

Uno then answered back, "I think there are 30 of them that are fairly complete."

"Did you say 30 of them?" Ray said as his jaw dropped in astonishment.

"Yeah, something like that, I'm tired of moving them around so I can mow the pasture." Uno stated. "I have them in my back pasture, people in the valley would bring their model T's to me so they wouldn't get used up in scrap metal drives during World War II. Thanks to old Henry Ford building them out of Vanadium steel, most of them are in pretty good shape. My neighbors always had a source for parts during the war. Now, everybody just wants to drive them cars with automatic transmissions and only two pedals. Nobody wants to drive a car with three pedals anymore. There are various models, in various states of running condition, would love to sell them all at one time. You can have the pile of miscellaneous parts if you buy all of them."

Ray was trying to take in what he just heard. He said, "Can I see them?"

"Ya sure, you betcha," Uno said. "Ya gotta watch out for the cowpies though, the cars are all in the back pasture."

Ray loved hearing that Finnish-American accent, it reminded him of his dad.

"I think I can dodge the cow pies, I really want to see these cars!" Ray said.

Ray and Uno walked over the hill to the pasture. It was like the heavens opened up and angels sang, there was a field filled with model T's in pretty good condition.

Most of them we're still on their wheels and tires, the ones that weren't, were sitting on wooden skids so Uno could move them around in the field with the doodlebug tractor. Almost all body styles were there, Fordors, runabouts, coupes, tourings, even a couple coupelets. The ones with fabric tops had canvas tarps covering them, so they were still in good shape.

Ray was seriously considering an early retirement, but this changed his mind. He asked Uno how much he wanted for the cars. Uno said "I want $50 each for those if you take them all, that sounds like a pretty fair price."

Without thinking twice, Ray stuck his hand out and said "You got a deal!"

"I need to head back home and get the money; I will pay you cash. What is your phone number? "Ray said.

Uno spoke up and said, "Don't have a phone at the house."

"Well then, what's your cell number?" Ray inquired.

"I already told you, if you buy them all, I'm selling them to you at $50 a car. Are you playing some sort of game with me?" Uno quickly answered back, sounding somewhat irritated.

Ray didn't want to press the issue, so he just said that he would line up some transport trucks and be back midweek if that was okay.

It was almost noon, so Ray and Uno walked back to Ray's Ford. They shook hands to complete the deal and then Uno said, "I see that you're driving Martin's car, when did he paint it?"

Ray's jaw dropped open again, he said "Do you know Martin?"

"Ya, I do, I see him every time I go to Rita's cafe." Uno said.

"Do you think he would be there now? Ray inquired.

"He should be, he opens up the place for Rita on Sunday mornings when she goes to church." Uno answered.

"Where is Rita's cafe?" Ray asked.

"Just stay on the main road going into Brooklyn, it's on the left-hand side. It's called 'Rita's Place'" Uno said.

Ray shook Uno's hand for the third time, and then thanked him for the information about Marty. Uno's speech was very much like his father, a typical Finnish-American accent and that made him feel comfortable. He was looking forward to seeing him again and hearing his voice when he came back. He just needed to find enough transport trucks to haul all the model T's back to Federal Way at one time.

Ray got into the Ford, crossed his fingers that it would start right up, and it did. This was a doubly amazing day, he found a treasure trove of model T's, and now he is on his way to see Marty.

Ray pulled into Brooklyn and didn't see any tavern, but he did see "Rita's Place", the cafe. He pulled up out front, and then caught a glimpse of Marty's Ford behind the cafe.

It was a typical small-town cafe with gingham curtains on the windows, probably a great place to get a good piece of homemade apple pie.

As he pushed the door open, a little bell at the top rang to let the staff know someone was here.

Ray could see Marty in the kitchen, cooking, facing away from the front counter.

Ray knew exactly how to introduce that he was there. Ray and Marty had both learned Morse code when they were in the Boy Scouts. When you were looking for someone with Morse code on a ham radio you would use the letters "C" and "Q". -"CQ" for "I seek you", which sounded like…

CHAPTER FIVE

"Dah-Di-Dah-Dit..."

"Dah-Di-Dah-Dit Dah-Dah-Di-Dah".... Which caused Marty to drop a bunch of pots and pans in the kitchen and making quite a racket.

Marty turned around and a big smile came to his face. "Ray Ray, I'm so glad you made it here!" They exchanged a quick hug and then the next thing Marty did was to check Ray's wrist.

It's not because he wanted to know what time it was, it was whether or not Ray held on to his Rolex. Ray thought that was strange, but he was glad to see Marty so it really didn't matter. The first thing Ray said was "What happened to you? You totally disappeared, the FBI has been hounding me monthly for information about you."

"It's a long story, let me buy you lunch, and when Rita shows up, we can take off for a while and I can explain. This is not the place to talk about it. Check out the calendar on the wall, I'm sure it will bring even more questions." Marty said. It was a calendar from a local service station called Fred's Super Shell in Artic, not that unusual, it just said that it's September 1955. There was no gas station in Artic, when he drove through on his way to the "Rod Run" Car Show on Friday. That made things even more mysterious.

Marty suggested the Blue Plate special, and whatever that was, is what Ray ordered. It was a good meal, and Ray was right, that place did make some pretty good homemade apple pie.

Ray was on his third cup of rather strong coffee when the bell over the door made its little ting-a-ling sound. In the door walked a beautiful lady that looked an awful lot like MaryAnn from Gilligan's Island. She had a yellow dress and a white pill box type hat on, it looked like she had just come there from church.

She spoke, and said "Marty, you have to see this, there's a car outside and it looks just like yours, only it's teal."

Marty said, "Yes ,I know, it belongs to my friend Ray Ray. I told you about him, he was my best friend in school. We were even in the Boy Scouts together". Marty then proceeded to make up a story about the cars. "We built our cars at the same time, that is why they look so much alike. These are the cars that we dreamed about.

We used to run around in Ray's beat up old model A in high school'.

Marty took off his apron and came around the lunch counter to introduce Ray to Rita.

"Rita, this is my best friend, Ray Ray. His mother called him Ray Ray because his dad was known as Big Ray". And then. "Ray, this is my best gal, Rita". Marty said.

Ray didn't know what to say other than "Congratulations Marty, you have an absolutely gorgeous, best gal". And "So this is why I haven't seen you the past year".

Marty motioned to Ray, behind Rita's back a slight "no" signal by moving his head back and forth. And then put his finger up to his lips as if to say "Shhh".

Marty then said to Rita, "Honey, I've got a bunch of catching up to do with Ray Ray, if you can handle the post-Church rush by yourself, I would like to visit with him for about an hour".

"Sure, I got it babe," Rita said. "Has it been busy this morning? "

"Nope, just the usual Sunday morning crowd of people trying to beat hangovers with strong coffee and apple pie". Marty answered.

Ray offered to pay for his delicious meal, but Marty said, "No, it's on me, your money's no good here". Which was true because Marty's money was absolutely no good there.

Marty quickly ushered Ray out the door, and to Ray's car.

Marty said, "Let's go for a drive, I have a lot to explain to you".

Ray asked Marty which direction he should go, and Marty said "Turn left out of here, let's head away from town". Ray crossed his fingers, hoping the Ford would start. That new battery was a great investment, because it fired right up.

"I have to ask you a question first, how long have I been gone? Because I am not exactly sure what is going on here". Marty said.

Ray thought that was a strange question to ask but he answered him "You have been gone exactly one year".

Marty then said, "Are you on the way back from "Rod Run"?

Ray answered "Yes".

"Well, that kind of confirms a suspicion of mine", Marty said. "Somehow, we got messed up in a time slip".

"We got what? What are you talking about? Marty, you gotta come clean with me". Ray said.

"Here is what I know, it's the year 1955, somehow we have slipped back more than 60 years in time. When I got here, it was 1954, and a calendar year has passed since then. I wasn't sure how time was passing where you were, but this lines up now".

"I was thinking I was either in a time slip, or a multiverse reality. Which still isn't out of the question, but not as likely."

"We are trapped in this place. This all started a year ago when I thought I would check out Brooklyn. I was driving over the North River Bridge and there was a sound of a large explosion. My car died, and then it started right up again once I crossed over the bridge.

Ray interrupted Marty, saying "The same thing happened to me. 1955? Really? This is some really weird Twilight Zone kind of stuff. Unless you're kidding me, please tell me you're kidding me."

"No, I am truly not kidding you." Marty answered.

"We are trapped here. You mean to tell me that we can't just drive back over the bridge, or in the opposite direction and be back in the present day?" Ray said.

"No, if you drive either direction you will be in the correct location, it'll be 1955 though." Said Marty. "You can drive west, and you will end up in

1955 Aberdeen, and if you drive east, you will eventually end up on Highway 99, and you can either go to 1955 Portland or Seattle. Interstate 5 won't even be started for another 3 years.".

"So, I am assuming that you have driven in both directions, more than once." Ray said.

"Yeah, I've been to Seattle a few times, and I go to Aberdeen to pick up supplies for the cafe every other week. I don't take my car because I have 1950 plates on it, and those are white and green, the wrong color, I would get pulled over right away."

"I am hesitant to go to Seattle though, I'm afraid that I may run into my parents or a relative and cause myself to not be born. I could really mess up the timeline there." Marty said.

Ray then said "I doubt that would happen, the Seahawks are still in Seattle, the Trailblazers are still in Portland, and the Space Needle is still in Spokane."

"Oh no! I messed up big time," said Marty. "I lost my souvenir Space Needle keychain somewhere on a trip to Seattle. Someone from Spokane must have picked it up, saw that as an idea, and somehow beat Seattle to building the Space Needle."

"But the Space Needle has always been in Spokane." Ray said. "We took a road trip there once in this car."

"No Ray, it was built in Seattle for the 1962 World's Fair. We used to go to the Space Needle and try to meet girls at the Fun Forest arcade at least once a month" Marty said. "Well, that's it, no more trips to Seattle to get equipment for the cafe, for me. As far as that matters, you shouldn't go there either, it's just too dangerous."

"Since it looks like you're going to be stuck here for an unknown amount of time like me, I need to print up some identification for you." Marty said.

"How are you going to do that? " Ray asked.

"Since you weren't going to Rod Run with me, I brought some work along, I have a laptop and a printer in the trunk of my car. Printing up a driver's license is no problem, in 1955 they were just printed on cardstock paper, I just used unprinted sections of menus from the cafe, to make mine. I scanned in a driver's license from a wallet that was left at the cafe, to get the fonts right."

"And since your car has 1954 plates on it, all we need to do is find a couple of the little silver metal tabs that slide in the slots on the plate that say "55" on them. You still have to make sure you never get pulled over though."

"Where am I going to stay?" Ray asked.

"You can just crash on my couch till we figure that out." Marty answered. "Once we get you some money, the one-bedroom place next to my little house rents for $18 a month. We should probably get you a fishing license. It will help you pass the time until we figure out some sort of job for you."

Ray said, "I could always find a job turning wrenches, being a mechanic, or working at a body shop somewhere."

"Unfortunately, there aren't any places like that in Brooklyn or Vesta, you could probably work at the service station out on Highway 101. Let's worry about that later though. We will get your identification printed up tonight. You will need it tomorrow, when we go into Aberdeen." Marty said.

Ray asked, "What are we going into Aberdeen for? How will we get money for me there?"

Marty pointed to the Rolex on Ray's wrist and said. "There is a pawn shop in Aberdeen that will give you $200 for that."

Ray immediately said, "$200 for my Rolex, this is worth several thousand!"

Marty answered, "Right now, it's 1955, and where else are you going to get money to survive on?"

To which Ray answered, "I guess you're right."

Marty then spoke up and said "I knew you were going to be here with me, we both received our watches on graduation day from a mysterious benefactor. The same one that undoubtedly funded our careers."

"I always wondered about the inscription on the back of our watches that said 'Keep me for all time and never go broke'" Ray said.

Marty then said, "If you haven't figured it out by now, we are our own mysterious benefactors. We figured out that the only way to have money in this time period is to carry something valuable on us. The Rolex watches are what we came up with. Obviously, any money we carried on ourselves would not be old enough to be able to be passed. Our Rolexes became our 'time-proof' banks on our wrists, and the best solution. We just need to figure out a way to be able to afford these watches now, so we will have them in the future. I pawned mine almost a year ago." Marty said. "We need to head back to the cafe; I need to see how Rita is doing. Why don't you head down to the North River, to see what kind of tackle people are using and find out if they're getting either steelhead or coho salmon, that'll give us an idea about what to buy for you tomorrow. And we will also pick up a fishing license for you.

Ray found a wide spot in the road, turned the Ford around, and headed back for Brooklyn. When they got to the cafe, there were several cars parked outside, so Marty said he better head back inside.

"Sorry babe," Marty said to Rita, "I had no idea it was going to get this busy."

"That's okay, it just got really busy a few minutes ago" said Rita, "did you have a good visit with your friend Ray Ray?"

"Yes I did," Marty answered. "He is doing some freelance writing for a fishing magazine, and he's here to fish the North River, and do some clam digging on the coast. He's looking for a place to stay here over the winter, and I told him about the little house next to mine."

"That would be nice," Rita said, "maybe you could go fishing with him and bring some salmon back to the cafe."

"That does sound like a lot of fun," Marty said, "but I hate to leave you here by yourself, at the cafe."

"I managed by myself before, I'm sure you would like a chance to get out of here occasionally." Rita said.

That was some quick thinking on Marty's part to come up with the idea of Ray being an outdoors writer who was looking for a place to stay over the winter. Ray was still going to have to find a place to work because there was no way that Marty could support him also. Marty only took a meager wage as a cook from Rita, to get by with. Who knows, maybe Ray could even write some articles and sell them.

When Marty first came through the time slip, he was pretty sure that he was in the past, just not exactly when. He was also pretty sure that he could not do anything that could change the future. He realized that this little community was the safest place for him to remain. He did not want to accidentally prevent his own birth.

He spotted Rita working outside a cafe that had not yet opened. There were sawhorses and lumber out front, he realized that this would be a chance to get a job.

Rita was dressed in work clothes and overalls, and she still looked gorgeous. He was definitely attracted to her; she was a total change from all the women that hung around him because he was rich. He liked the idea that she was obviously a person with a serious work ethic. He introduced himself to Rita and asked if she needed any help building the cafe. She told him that she had it pretty much figured out and was doing most of the work herself, but could use some help with the electrical wiring. Marty said "I'm your man, I worked as an electrician's assistant while going through college. I also worked as a cook if you're looking for one of those."

Marty helped Rita with the construction and completed all the electrical work. His work passed all the electrical inspections which made Rita very happy.

Rita also liked Marty's quiet and serious demeanor. They were alike in many ways. It was like the cosmos had found two people that were looking for each other, but didn't know that. Rita, in her early 40's, and Marty, in his early 50's, found that love that some people never do.

Marty was not sure if he wanted to return to the present day, he had found love in a much simpler existence. He had plenty of money in the present day, and no wants in this world. But now he knew life was more than that.

CHAPTER SIX

"Tick, Tick, Tick"

Ray spent the afternoon talking to the local fishermen and then went back to the cafe at closing time. Marty had put together a couple of "to-go" meals so that he and Ray could eat at his place. They unloaded a couple of cardboard boxes from the back of Marty's car and put them into the cafe's pickup truck. Marty was driving the cafe's pickup truck because he still needed to get the correct license plates for his car. Ray followed Marty to his little house.

Marty's place was one of a row of little square millworkers houses. They were all one bedroom houses, built during a more prosperous time. The house next to Marty's had a "for rent" sign in it, saying that the rent was $18 a month. Ray looked at the sign, and was glad about that. It was something he would be able to afford.

They brought the food and the two cardboard boxes into Marty's house. Marty made sure the curtains were shut before he unboxed the laptop and the printer. He would have a hard time explaining this technology in 1955.

The guys enjoyed their meal, and then got to work making a driver's license for Ray. The menus just happened to be the right color, and they showed some wear on them. They looked like they had been sitting in a wallet for a long time. Marty called up the driver's license he had scanned into the computer and changed the identification to Ray's name. Since Ray's car had Benton County plates on it, he just made up an address in Kennewick. 3rd Street is the most common address in America, so he just chose a number at random and gave him a 3rd Street address.

Marty printed it out, and it looked perfect. Now to come up with a backstory for Ray. One of the most important things was what did he do during World War II?

Ray and Marty tossed around several ideas, and came up with the idea that he was a Jeep driver and bodyguard for a colonel in the Army. That would explain how he avoided combat duty, and since Ray was a fairly muscular person, being a bodyguard made sense. That would also explain him living in Kennewick, he was a guard at the Hanford Nuclear Reservation. He was tired of living there, and just wanted to move to the coast and do some fishing. This all made sense, and that's what the guys decided to go with.

Marty's backstory, at least the one he went with, was that he was a communications specialist in the Air Force. That would explain his knowledge of electrical stuff. Also, he said that he went to college on the G.I. Bill.

Now to figure out when they built these cars. It had to be sometime before 1954 and obviously sometime after 1950. Cars were scarce post-war, and whatever they came up with had to make sense.

Fortunately, Marty had never discussed building his car with Rita. They came up with the idea that these were a couple of old county vehicles they bought at auction. The story is that they both were still living with their parents in King county. After discharge from the military in 1951.

Ray took a job at the Hanford Nuclear Reservation as a guard, and Marty drifted from job to job, looking for the right one.

Ray was glad to have found Marty after a year of worry about him. Now he just worried about his mother and his dog "Molly", and would he ever get to see them again. Then there was Mary, as much resistance as he put up, he kind of liked her and her spirit. If he ever made it back, he promised himself that he would spend some time getting to know her.

Marty brought Ray a pillow and a quilt so he could have a good night's sleep. The couch was fairly comfortable to sleep on.

In the quiet of the room, Ray listened to the tick, tick, tick, of his beloved Rolex he had for so many years, knowing that he was going to pawn it tomorrow.

His Rolex had always been part of his life, he got it as one of two stipulations from a mysterious benefactor. He always had to wear the Rolex, and never go to New York.

The mysterious benefactor gave Marty enough money for 6 years of college, and for Ray to build his own shop.

It was just today that he realized that Marty and he were their own mysterious benefactors. Neither the two boys or their parents knew where the money came from.

And then it hit him, the message wasn't don't go to New York, it was don't go to Brooklyn. In his cross USA tour last year with Invictus, he skipped exhibiting at the car shows in New York. He could have gone, oh well.

The cafe was closed on Mondays, and it was Marty's day to go into Aberdeen to pick up food supplies for the week. Rita and Marty would alternate doing the Monday supply runs, so at least every other week they could have one day off from the cafe.

Marty got up around 7:00 a.m. and made some bacon and scrambled eggs for breakfast. It really hit the spot for Ray, Marty was actually a pretty decent cook.

The laptop and the printer were boxed up last night, and ready to go into the truck.

Marty and Ray headed for the cafe to put the boxes back in the trunk of the car, and to pick up the list of what was needed from Aberdeen. Marty put the boxes away, double checked that he locked the trunk, and got back in the truck with Ray.

When they got to Highway 101 on the way to Aberdeen, the first thing Ray noticed was the road was much narrower, and there were power poles on both sides of the road. He had just driven this road on Friday, it was much wider, and all the power was underground. He made a note to himself to never underestimate all the work done on a highway that a person never sees.

The first town you come to is Cosmopolis, and a big Weyerhaeuser mill on the right-hand side of the street. The mill wasn't there when he drove through on Friday. He thought about all the people working there in 1955, and the loss of all those jobs in the present day. Progress is sometimes very painful.

Marty pulled the truck into the parking lot of the pawn shop. He asked Ray "Are you ready?"

Ray answered, " As much as I will ever be."

They went inside, and Ray managed to get $250 for his Rolex. He immediately spent some of the money buying a tackle box and a couple fishing poles. The next stop was a sporting goods store for a fishing license, some fishing tackle, and a clam shovel. The fake driver's license worked very well at the pawn shop, and when he needed to get his fishing license.

The next stop was picking up supplies for the cafe, which went fairly fast.

They were getting ready to leave back for Brooklyn when they realized that Ray did not have a typewriter to write his fishing stories, so they headed back to the pawn shop where they found a Remington typewriter in pretty good shape. He also picked up a Kodak brownie camera for a few dollars, to photograph the fish that people were catching.

This trip back to the pawn shop was a reminder to them that they needed to be aware of their total story. And especially to not forget any of the details. A writer needs a typewriter.

They also stopped at the Woolworth's and picked up some bedding, towels, and kitchenware for Ray's little house. There was one more stop, for paper for the typewriter, and film for the camera. So far, Ray had spent almost $150 of his $250, and he had not even bought groceries. When he got back to Brooklyn, he needed to get that rental house, and start looking for a job right away.

CHAPTER SEVEN

"Let me check your oil"

Ray contacted the landlord and rented the place next to Marty that afternoon and paid his first and last month's rent. That will make Ray's life a lot simpler. At least for now.

Ray's heart was not in settling down in 1955. He wanted to go home. He wanted to see his mother again. He wanted to take his puppy dog for a walk. He wanted to make sure his employees were taken care of. These were things he could not do stuck in 1955. Ray realized all the people that were depending on him, and that they had to be as worried about him, as he was about Marty when he disappeared.

Ray was not sure that Marty even wanted to go back to current day, he had a best gal there in 1955, after all. Ray and Marty had been friends for over 40 years, and they had always been honest with each other.

When they got back to Brooklyn, Marty put the groceries in the freezer of the cafe, and then dropped Ray off at his house. Ray pretty much had his house all in order that Monday afternoon. Ray's plan that evening was to confront Marty about his intention to stay in 1955, or go home to present day.

Ray and Marty had dinner together at Marty's place that evening. After dinner, Marty suggested to Ray that they should make up a fake registration for his car in case he gets pulled over. He figured that he would scan in the registration from Rita's car to get the fonts correct.

At this point, Ray decided it was time to ask Marty if he ever intended on going back to the present day.

"Marty, are you going to stay here? I want to get home as soon as possible; I have a lot of people depending on me. If you plan on staying, that is fine, but please help me get home." Ray implored.

"It's not like I don't have people depending on me either, back there," Marty said. "My brother is competent enough to run the company by himself. At least I hope he is."

"Your company is doing fine," Ray answered. "Your employees are being well taken care of. Your wisdom once again shows through, I'm glad that you asked me to be on the board of directors. I have been able to keep an eye on your company and help guide it in a positive direction in your absence. And your brother is a very competent leader. It has been a year since you disappeared, so he has called together a meeting of the board of directors in 3 weeks to discuss the future of the company. From my conversations with him, I have found out that he never expected to be the CEO of the company. I fear that is overwhelming him, and he might move to put the company up for sale. I also sense that some of the directors on the board are chomping at the bit to take over the company.

Marty said "I really don't want to see the company sold, but it would leave my brother set up for life, he would never have to work again. I'm sure that he will take care of our parents, I also left a sizable portion of my holdings to my sister, she will never have to worry either."

"It sounds like you are planning to stay here," Ray said.

"I think so," Marty said. "I love that Rita has such a pioneer spirit, she reminds me a lot of me. That doesn't mean that I won't help you get home."

"That is what I was hoping to hear," Ray said. "Just please don't do anything to prevent my birth."

Marty said, "It's a deal! I will do my best to stay away from the Seattle area."

Ray immediately spoke up, "We need to figure out what has triggered our time slip. Our cars must be the key to what happened. We just need to figure out why, and can we reverse it?"

Marty said, "I agree with you that it must be the cars that are triggering it, because we have not seen anyone else from the future. At least, I haven't. I have been looking for people that have seemed out of place, and not seen anyone beside you."

"Maybe we came through some sort of weather anomaly. What was the weather like when you crossed the bridge near Vesta? Marty said.

It was a beautiful sunny Sunday morning, of course it was foggy/steamy by the river. I remember seeing what I thought was steam or fog coming off the river. Ray said.

"I had the same weather when my time slip occurred," Marty answered. "It sounds like if you want to return to the present day, you will have to do it on a sunny morning that is warm enough to have fog/steam coming off the river."

"I heard people talking at the cafe that we are supposed to have sunny weather for the next few days, that should give you several shots at getting home." Marty said.

Sounds great to me." Ray said. "I'm going to put a job application in at the Shell station in Artic tomorrow. Hopefully, I will go home and not make it to Artic at all."

We also need to get some of the silver "55" metal tabs that slide onto your license plate to bring your 1954 license plate up to date. Marty said. "You are so lucky that's all you need for your plates to look current. Having the 1950 plates on my car has been such a hassle. I had to make up a phony bill of sale from someone, so I could apply for a "lost title" on my car. But at least when I get a new title, I will have a car with good plates on it. I'm sure glad I didn't go with modern vanity plates on the car, there's no way I could explain those."

Marty and Ray finished up the evening talking about both of their back stories, making sure they matched.

Ray got up the next morning around 8:00 a.m. and loaded the stuff he brought to the car show in his Ford. He figured that he would try driving over the bridge several times over the next couple hours. If there was steam/fog around the river, he figured he had a shot at getting home.

Unfortunately, after about a dozen tries, the fog burned away. Today was not the day he was going to go home, Ray realized. Maybe tomorrow.

There was nothing more to do now other than to drive to Fred's Super Shell station to see if there was a job.

Ray was dressed in his normal clothes, blue jeans and a heavy black button-down work shirt. Ideal for a job at a service station.

Ray pulled into the station and found Fred working on a Plymouth. He introduced himself and asked if there were any openings for a mechanic.

Fred said that he didn't need a mechanic, but certainly could use a "pump jockey" (the guy that works the gas pumps). Fred let him know that the pay was above minimum wage, it was $1.10 an hour. Ray countered Fred's offer saying that he would take seventy five cents an hour and a percentage of whatever he sold. Fred hired him on the spot and went back to work on the Plymouth.

Ray sold two sets of tires, a couple oil changes, a job to replace a water pump, and several sets of wiper blades that afternoon. He was on his way to making over $400 his first week, and Fred's shop had never been busier.

Perhaps Ray didn't have to write about fishing at all.

Ray was a natural at saying "Let me check your oil." And then pointing out everything that was needed for the car.

This was kind of fun for Ray cuz he enjoyed working on 1940's and 1950's automobiles. It was a shame that all these cars were stuck in 1955 because he sure would like to bring a lot of them back to the present day. Especially all those model T's that he saw yesterday. If only he could bring them home.

Ray realized that he needed to stop by the old guy's house that had the model T's and let him know that he was not going to get them.

He pulled up behind the Fordor sedan and got out of his car. He went up and knocked on the old guy's door. When the old guy came out, he could see the disappointment and Ray's face, and knew the sale was off. Ray was not the first person that said he was going to buy the cars, and then back out. Ray was the first person though to tell him to his face that things were not working out, and he was going to end up staying in Brooklyn. The old guy appreciated Ray's honesty.

Ray once again thanked the old guy for telling him where Marty was. He also told him how much he liked hearing the Finnish-American accent again, and how it reminded him of his dear departed father.

Ray's honesty ended up making him a friend, when it very well could have gone the opposite direction.

Despite having a frustrating morning, and not being able to trigger the reverse time slip, he had a very productive afternoon at the service station, and made a new friend with Uno, the old guy.

CHAPTER EIGHT

"It's lantern time"

That night Marty and Ray were having dinner together at Marty's house, and discussing Ray's day, and his efforts to go to the present time. Marty spoke up and said, "That's exactly what I did, I can't tell you how many times I drove across that bridge. I was pretty sure that the Lakes pipes and the tune of the engine set off some sort of harmonic vibration that caused the time slip. And that the foggy / steamy air coming up from the river was the catalyst. I am sure there is something simple that we are overlooking. We just need to figure out what that is."

"I'm glad that you became friends with Rita's uncle Uno, he is a bit of a curmudgeon, but he's a pretty nice guy," Marty said.

"Uno is Rita's uncle?" Ray asked.

"Yeah, he is the person that gave her the building the cafe is in," Marty said. "Rita had been working at a cafe in Raymond when Uno offered her the building. It used to be a general store, and since everyone now shops in either Raymond or Aberdeen now, it went out of business."

"Rita embodies the strong-willed, stoic personality trait that the Finnish call 'sisu.'" Uno knew that Rita would make the cafe work." Marty said.

Ray said, "My mother always used to say 'sisu' means 'bullheaded.'"

Marty laughed so hard that he almost fell out of his chair. "Well, that's true too." Marty said.

Marty then asked Ray how his day at Fred's Super Shell went. "I am doing pretty well, I am on track to make about $400 this week, I made a deal with Fred to get a percentage of whatever I sold. I seem to be doing pretty good at that." answered Ray.

"That is fantastic," said Marty, "We need to build up our finances so we can be our own benefactors. We don't need to make all the money now, but we will need to contact a lawyer to make investments for us, since it will be several years before we are even born. Unless we choose a young lawyer, there's a good chance he may not be around long enough to make all the correct investments. We will be at his mercy that he follows our instructions, it will need to be profitable for him too. Does that make sense to you? "Marty said. "It sounds like you thought this out, what investments are we going to make and how will you know how to make them?"

"I have realized that technology is a very volatile industry, and I have wanted my company to survive. Do you remember Radio Shack, Netscape, Circuit City, America Online. Compaq, Palm?" Marty said.

"Palm? What's that? "Ray asked.

"The Palm pilot, do you remember that?" Marty answered.

"Oh yeah I do, never had one though," said Ray. "What would all these failed giant companies have to do with us?"

"I have been studying all these failures so I can keep my business alive. I have several Kindle books on my laptop explaining when these and several non-tech companies grew, clear back into the 1950s, what happened to them, and why they failed. If we can invest in companies early enough before they become large, and then sell before they collapse, we stand to make a large amount of money." Marty explained.

"What about messing with the timeline, won't our investments cause a repercussion? Ray inquired.

"No, I don't think so, we will never make that large of an investment to significantly make any difference on the timeline. At least I hope not. Marty answered.

"Now the tough question," Ray said. "Where do we find an honest lawyer?"

"Well, I guess it's time for us to get out our lantern," Marty said.

"Our lantern?" Ray asked.

"Do you remember the story of the Greek philosopher Diogenes, who carried around a lantern during the day looking for an honest man?" Marty said.

"Well, I guess it's lantern time," said Ray.

"I'm thinking that we need to either look in Raymond or Aberdeen for a lawyer," said Marty. "The smaller we keep our circle of influence, the better it will be. I don't think we dare contact a lawyer in Olympia or Seattle.

Changing the subject, Ray asked "If I find a way to get back home, will you continue to build our nest egg?"

"Absolutely." said Marty. "This time slip thing is quite confusing, and I still don't know if we just didn't end up in a parallel multiverse. We could still be in the present day, it's just that the world we are in has only progressed to what we know as 1955."

The guys called it an early evening, and Ray went back to his house. Ray's head was spinning trying to take in all the information that Marty had imparted to him. Ray thought, "What if this was a parallel multiverse? Would anything they're doing even make a difference?"

Ray turned on the radio in his house hoping to get some sort of clue to what was going on in this world today, but instead he found the Mitch Miller Orchestra playing "The Yellow Rose of Texas."

"That was absolutely no help," Ray thought. "Guess I need to get the lantern out in the morning."

As Ray was getting ready for bed, thoughts of his mother, his dog, and his crew at the shop, kept running through his head. He said a quick prayer and crawled into bed.

Ray got up early and was ready to do several trips across the Vesta bridge. Ray was thinking the time slip happened because he slowed down to an almost stop because of the fog.

Ray fixed himself a quick breakfast of cold cereal, he wanted to get out to that bridge as soon as possible.

Ray was hoping that he would hit upon the secret that would send him back home this morning. But today was going to be another day of disappointment, he was still in 1955. After 8 passes across the bridge, again. It was just like the day before.

Ray kept running over all the possibilities of how the time slip happened and he came upon a couple ideas.

He was pretty sure that Marty's idea of the Lakes pipes and the exhaust sound had something to do with it. On top of that, the 1950 Ford with its shoebox flat body side design makes a perfect reflector for the exhaust.

He remembered that the flathead motor would cause static on his parents television set; he was wondering if the RFI (radio frequency interference) was part of the equation. It had to be the way the spark plugs were mounted on the cylinder head of the motor.

By the time Ray got to work, he was pretty sure that the inherent RFI of the flathead motor, plus the exhaust tone coming out of the Lakes pipes and reflecting off the flat sides of the body were the cause.

These three things are probably why no other vehicles have come through from future times.

This was something that he needed to discuss with Marty that evening.

It was another busy day at Fred's Super Shell

Service. Ray even managed to get a logging company account for the station to take care of the tires on its trucks. Fred just needed to invest in some equipment to service large tires. Fred was very happy with this setup; he could make good money on large tires. Ray even got the tire distributor to sell Fred tires at a lower price. Not bad for day two on the job. Unfortunately, he had zero luck in finding a lawyer in all the customers he had that day.

Ray's duties that afternoon included going to Fred's impound lot behind the station, where Fred hauled all the wrecked cars to. He spotted a car that had the license tabs that he needed for the Ford. He asked Fred if he could have the "55" (year) tabs off of it, as someone stole his, and Fred said that was fine with him, as he was very happy with everything Ray had been doing for the station. Besides, the wreck was going to be crushed in a couple days. That night after work, Ray retrieved the two metal tabs and put them on his license plates. At least, the Ford looked legal now.

Marty brought his laptop and printer home that evening and they made a fake registration for Ray's car.

Ray was in pretty good shape at this point,

with these two little metal tabs, he had current plates on his car, a car registration (albeit fake), and a driver's license (albeit fake). He should be able to pass a superficial inspection by a police officer, hopefully that is enough. The guys packed up the laptop and the printer into their cardboard boxes as soon as they finished, in case Rita showed up. That technology would be pretty hard to explain.

Ray talked with Marty that night about his suspicion that the RFI from the engine, plus Marty's idea of the exhaust tone coming out of the Lakes pipes were the triggers of the time slip.

The RFI part of the equation made sense to Marty, and the part about the flat sides of the car reflecting the sound seemed logical.

The guys discussed how the weather was beautiful on those Sunday mornings of the time slip, and that they had both front windows rolled down. Perhaps that was it. Maybe, with the windows open, the exhaust resonance was the final trigger point. Ray decided the following morning that he would drive across the bridge with both front windows down, to see if that would work.

Ray woke up the next morning to a typical, coastal Washington State, gray sky. He was wondering if the good weather window had passed him this year. He just needed another sunny morning to find out if the open windows were the key to going home.

Ray packed his fishing gear in the back of the Ford, and went into work early, figuring he would go fishing later in the afternoon.

Day number four of 1955, or whenever or wherever he was, was uneventful. A perfect day to take off early and go fishing.

Ray made it down to the North River, and where he decided to cast his line in the water, there was only one other fisherman there. The other guy appeared to be about half of Ray's age, and already had one coho salmon laying on the bank.

Ray struck up a conversation with this young man to find out what he was fishing with. Ray and the young man talked about what bait to use on this section of the river. On Ray's first cast, he came up with a fairly large coho. He went over to thank the young man and asked him if he fished the North River a lot. The young man said that he had not been able to do much fishing as he just finished law school and was getting ready to take his bar exam. He said that upon passing, he would set up a practice in Aberdeen. His family lived there, and he wanted to stay close to them.

Ray was flabbergasted, did he just find the (almost a) lawyer he was looking for? He then realized that he had not introduced himself to the young man. "My name is Ray, Ray Raittinen, I apologize for not introducing myself earlier." Ray said. The young man said "Hello Ray, my name is Pete, Pete Johnson."

"I work out on the highway at Fred's Super Shell, stop by sometime. I will make sure your car is well taken care of when you get gas." said Ray. "I have some financial legal questions that I would like to discuss with you at some time in the future." Ray added.

"I can't do anything until I pass my bar exam, which is coming up next week. Let me write my phone number down for you, I don't have any business cards yet," Pete said.

Pete's conversation stopped short because he had another fish on the line. It was another coho, and that limited out Pete for the day. Overall, it was a pretty good day, Pete caught a couple fish, and Ray caught one, and a (almost) lawyer too! He didn't even need a lantern. Ray's business intuition told him that Pete was the guy Marty and him were looking for.

CHAPTER NINE

"I'll have the Blue Plate Special"

Ray stopped by the cafe and gave the salmon to Rita, as he really didn't have the right stuff to cook it properly.

He talked with her and said he appreciated her sharing Marty over the past three nights so they could get caught up with old times. As he listened to Rita, he was picking up that Finnish-American accent that he hadn't noticed earlier. He could see why Marty was so enthralled with her, in addition to the accent that Ray loved to hear, he could tell in the way that Rita spoke that she truly did have a pioneer spirit.

Ray grabbed a spot at the lunch counter and ordered the Blue Plate Special, with apple pie, of course. Marty had been pretty busy in the kitchen and didn't have a chance to talk with Ray.

Ray lifted his hand up and made a motion to Marty, like he was carrying a lantern, and then did a quick switch to a thumbs up gesture.

Marty returned the thumbs up gesture to Ray, and then motioned that they would talk later that evening. Ray then headed back to his house.

Ray was pretty bummed that he did not get any passes over the bridge that morning. He felt confident that he was getting closer to reversing the time slip, but there was just something simple he was missing. He hoped the weather would be better in the morning so he could try the "windows down" theory that Marty and he talked about.

Marty showed up at Ray's house about 9:00 that evening.   Ray told him about Pete, the lawyer he met that day. At least, very soon to be a lawyer, that he felt he could trust. Ray conveyed to Marty that he was worried because he had no idea how he could convince Pete to make these needed investments. Marty had already thought that through. Marty said "We simply tell him the truth, that we are from the future."

"Are you crazy?" Ray said, "There is no way he is going to believe us."

"He will if we show him some proof," Marty said.

"What proof can we show him? We certainly can't show him the laptop and printer. He could take those from us." Ray said.

"We have our cell phones, they won't work as a phone, but they will work as a still camera and a movie camera. We can take pictures or a movie of him" Marty said. "If we have pictures on our phones from the present day that will give him a look into what the future looks like. We will explain to him this is also a communication device that does not work at the moment because the network does not exist yet. Only we'll call it something like home base because he most likely won't understand what the word network means. We can also show him whatever apps we have installed on our phones; these should totally blow his mind."

Ray said, "We need to make sure that he is isolated from other people when we explain this, I would hate to have someone eavesdrop on that conversation."

"I will figure out when to invest in what stocks, and give him a different envelope for every year, with instructions." Marty said. "His instructions will explain that he only opens that year's envelope, or everything could fall apart. We will pay him a percentage of our profits from the stock purchases, he will also be free to invest along with us, if he chooses. He will also be given instructions to purchase a matching pair of pre-

1955 Rolexes for both of us from the proceeds and have them engraved with 'Keep me for all time and never go broke'. All monies earned for us will go into an irrevocable trust he sets up for us, and to be paid off to us upon our graduation from high school. It will be up to him to figure out all the legal details. I hope we make him a very rich man. I am only concerned about the watches, and the amount of money required for my college education, and for you to open your shop. He will have to give us the stipulations that we always wear our watch, and we never go to Brooklyn.

Ray said, "I'm not sure how this time slip or multiverse thing works, hopefully this next time around they get it straight and not say 'Never go to New York'."

"When should we have our meeting with Pete?" Ray asked.

"I'm thinking pretty soon," said Marty. "At least I will need to meet him, if you manage to go home, and I stay behind.

If I stay here, I will be able to help guide them to our financial goal. Marty said.

"If you stay here? Are you thinking about changing your mind, and going back to the present day?" Ray asked.

If I could bring Rita back with me, I would consider coming back. I'm just not sure if Rita would survive a reverse time slip, it could age her 60+ years in just one moment. Marty said. "She would be over 100 years old, and most likely not survive the reverse time slip."

"Do you mean we could possibly age 60 plus years on a return trip to the present day?" Ray inquired.

"That is always a possibility," Marty said, "I still don't know if we're in a time slip or a parallel multiverse."

Ray said, "Well, that's a risk I definitely want to take. I miss Mom, Molly, and the guys at the shop, and the more I see you and Rita together, I think I may even miss Mary a little bit."

"Mary? Who is that?" Marty asked.

"She is a gal by the name of Mary, I built a '56 Chevy Nomad for her. She has a variety of unique cars, and races some of them. I think she is about Rita's age, and she's pretty good looking. She is tall, has blue eyes and long blonde hair, and she is one smart lady. I see some of the pioneer woman spirit in her, that you do in Rita. Even though she is not Finnish, she very much has 'sisu'. And for some reason that I don't understand, she is interested in me, and I'm a good 10 years older than her.

"She sounds like a wonderful lady," Marty said. "Does that mean you will finally settle down when you go back?"

"I have been contemplating retirement the past couple years, I built all the great projects that I wanted. I believe that being with Mary could lead my life to new adventures. I sure hope that time travel is not part of any newer adventures though," said Ray. "Right now, all I want to do is concentrate on going home. I understand that the weather is supposed to be good tomorrow, I will be out there early, making passes across the bridge. Hope I don't see you tomorrow evening." Ray said with a chuckle in his voice.

Marty and Ray said their good nights to each other like they had the past few evenings. But now there was the possibility that Ray was going home and he would never see Marty again.

CHAPTER TEN

"Born on a mountaintop in Tennessee"

Ray got up early the next morning to beautiful weather, he was so ready to drive over that bridge.

When he got to the bridge, he noticed that the bottom of the side door windows matched up to the top of the ledge of the bridge. "This has to be it," he thought. He was frustrated that he had not remembered that he had both windows open when he crossed over the bridge. The steam / fog was exactly like it was when he made the time slip. He crossed his fingers and made his first pass across the bridge. He drove a little further until he saw a car with the green license plates, which meant he was still in 1955. Ray went back and made another seven passes back and forth, across that bridge. Every time he crossed it, he was still in 1955.

Perhaps this was a one-way trip, and he would never get home. His gut feeling told him otherwise, and he was not going to stop trying, maybe he needed to attempt a return home trip in the spring. Hopefully it wouldn't take that long, but he was going to try every day the river was warm enough to let off the steam/fog that surrounded his car on that fateful day. Ray gave up for the day and headed into work. It was another uneventful day at Fred's Super Shell Service. Ray went home that night feeling very dejected. He was sure that he duplicated everything that he did when the time slip happened back on Sunday.

Then it occurred to him that he had the radio on. He was listening to what the announcer said was arguably the first rock and roll song ever, it was something about an Oldsmobile he just couldn't remember the name of the song. The lyrics were something about everybody in the car "taking a trip and oozing and cruising and getting a beer." Or something like that.

He had to talk with Marty about that. Did Marty have his radio on, and if so, what was he listening to?

Marty showed up late that evening, just to check in on Ray. He spent most of his evening with Rita, he did not want to jeopardize his relationship.

Ray couldn't wait to talk to Marty about the music. Ray was pretty sure that it was the last piece of the puzzle. Of course, that's what he thought about the windows being rolled down too.

"Marty, were you listening to the radio when your time slip happened, and what was playing on the radio if it was on?" Ray said with such speed that Marty didn't understand it. Ray took a breath and then slowly repeated himself.

Marty said as a matter of fact "I did have my radio on, it was some Sunday morning syndicated program, and it was playing Jackie Brenston's Rocket 88. The only reason I remember it is because the announcer said that it was the first rock and roll record."

"They had to have been repeating the same program from a year ago because I remember the announcer saying the same thing," said Ray. "I will be ready to drive across the bridge tomorrow morning, if you can call into a radio station and request that song for me."

"It makes sense to me, as much as any of this time slip has, I will call into the radio station tomorrow at 8:00 a.m." Marty said. Ray finally felt good, he was pretty sure this was going to take him home. He was looking forward to seeing his mom, his dog, and the crew at the shop, again. Ray stopped by the cafe at 7:30 the next morning, to see if Marty was ready to make that phone call.

He figured he would probably have to wait until his song came up in the queue. It would be best if Marty called about 7:45 a.m. He headed straight for the bridge and turned his radio on. Marty got the phone number for the radio station in Aberdeen's request line. The disc jockey came on and asked him what his request was, and he said he would like to hear "Rocket 88" by Jackie Brenston. The disc jockey immediately said "We don't play no colored music here. This is a station for us white folks."

"But I just bought a new Oldsmobile, and I would really like to hear this song," Marty said.

"There are no 'race' stations anywhere on the coast," the DJ said.

"What?" said Marty.

"I said there are no stations for people of the black race on the coast," said the DJ.

Marty was totally flabbergasted by the DJ saying this. He knew that African Americans were discriminated against in 1955, he had no idea they had to have separate radio stations though. He went totally silent on the phone; this was not right.

The DJ said, "Hello, Hello, I will see what I can do for you.   Marty hung up the phone, he was part angry, and part in disbelief.

In the meantime, Ray was parked and waiting at the bridge. He heard the DJ say that a request from Marty would be coming up after the commercial.

Ray started up the Ford and waited for the piano intro, which was his cue to pull onto the bridge. The DJ came back on the air and said "Unfortunately, I cannot find Marty's request, so I will play this hour's most requested song."

"Oh no," thought Ray. "Whatever this is, I sure hope it works." And then the song started- "Born on a mountain top in Tennessee, the greenest state in the land of the free." Ray recognized the tune, it was "The Ballad of Davy Crockett".

Ray figured he might as well pull onto the bridge since he was there, he hoped it wouldn't put him further back in time. Just like all his other attempts, he crossed over the bridge, and was in 1955.

Ray waited and attempted crossings with the next couple songs, but neither of them worked.

Ray drove back to the cafe, and asked Marty what happened. Marty explained that "Rocket 88" would only be played on a "race" station in 1955. Ray was in shock, and also in anger at the treatment of human beings in 1955. At that moment, they both decided that regardless of whether they are stuck in 1955 or make it to the present day, they will do their best to make this world a better place. Obviously, it was time for a "plan B" of some sort. How were they going to get this song played on a radio station that they could receive in Brooklyn.

Ray asked Marty if he had any ideas on a way to amplify a signal from either Portland or Seattle.

Marty said he would see if any of the ham radio equipment that he purchased recently could work as a repeater. Marty was always playing around with ham radio stuff, and he was enjoying all the old tube radios that he was picking up for next to nothing. He had not got his ham radio license for a couple reasons, one was that he would have to prove who he was, and that wasn't easy, and he also didn't want to mess up the timeline. Which he could really do if he was talking internationally. He had been picking up various equipment from people that were selling it in the local newspaper.

Marty spent most of the day drawing out diagrams for a repeater, when the answer hit him.

He was pretty sure that he could just use his Ham radios and transmit in the AM Radio band. He would just need a copy of the record, and a record turntable that he could wire up to the radio. While what he was doing was illegal, he would not need to transmit more than just the length of the song, and then shut the radio down. It was time to get the Sears catalog out and order a record turntable with an output jack. Fiddling around with one of his ham radios to transmit on the original frequency they heard the song on, was just a matter of a couple hours of work. And since that radio station was not in existence yet, it would not be a problem transmitting at that frequency.

Marty found a magazine that listed records for sale. He figured he should probably buy three copies of the record in case one or two of them got damaged. He immediately sent out a money order for the records, he hoped he would receive those shortly. The Sears automatic turntable was $29.95, and with the 45 RPM records only being 49 cents each the total expenditure came to $34 with shipping. Marty thought that was a pretty good deal.

With this figured out, it was imperative that the guys needed to contact the soon-to-be lawyer, Pete Johnson. Ray was most likely going to be going home soon.

CHAPTER ELEVEN

"Strong coffee and apple pie"

Now, it was just a waiting game for the turntable, and the records. Ray got his first check from Fred and immediately reimbursed Marty for the $34. Ray had a little bit of financial breathing room now that he cashed the first check.

Ray took that Sunday off work. Lord knows Fred would love to have had him at the station. The weekends see a lot of traffic on Highway 101, and the station is always busy. Ray went to the cafe for that Sunday morning strong coffee and apple pie, which the cafe was famous for.

Marty was busy in the kitchen all morning, so Ray just waved to him and motioned that he was going fishing.

Ray got down to the river and Pete was already down there. This was a perfect time to talk with him, as there were no other people at the river. He had his cell phone charged up, and he was ready to blow Pete's mind with some future technology. Ray saw that Pete had a fish on his line, so he got out his cell phone and videoed it. It was another beautiful coho salmon that Pete got.

Ray walked up to him and asked if he remembered him from the other day and Pete said "yes." Ray said, "I have something to show you. I have a video of you landing that salmon."

"You have a what?" Pete asked.

"A video," said Ray, "it's kind of like a short little movie."

Ray pulled the cell phone out of his pocket and showed the video to Pete.

"What is that thing?" Pete asked.

"It is a camera," Ray answered.

"I figured that much," said Pete. "Is it just a movie camera, will it work with a projector, and where did you get it?"

"Well," said Ray, "it also takes still pictures. Hold up that fish and let me take a picture of you."

Pete picked up the salmon, and Ray took a picture of him. Ray showed him the picture, and Pete asked "Where does the film go in this camera? I don't even see a place big enough to hold a roll of film."

"That's because this is an electronic camera, and it doesn't use film." Ray said. "And it will work with an electronic projector if you wish to show the little movies on a big screen."

"Is this something from the military? Where did you get this thing from?" Pete asked.

Ray said "No, it's not from the military, I need you to be open-minded, can you do that?"

"Well, you certainly have my attention, college did teach me one thing and that was to be open-minded, and to get all the facts," said Pete.

"I am from about 65 years in the future, I am not sure how or why I landed here, or if I will be able to go back home. I could use some help from you." Ray said.

"From me?" Asked Pete.

"Yes from you." Ray answered.

"First thing," Pete asked, "Where are you from, and why do you need me?"

"I am from Washington State, a town called Federal Way where I have a car kustomizing shop, I need you to make investments for me, it will be for my future use, and if you want, it can make you a very rich man."

"I built a couple of cars that, unknown to me, were time travel machines, that sent my friend Marty and me back to this time. I desperately want to go home."

Pete was now holding Ray's cell phone and looking it over, Ray showed him pictures of cars that he took at car shows the previous year. Some of these were cars that would not be built for another 50 years. Some were custom cars; some were unmodified cars. Also on his phone's photo album, there were many pictures of landmarks and buildings from his cross-country trip with Invictus.

At this point, Pete said that he needed to sit down, this was too much for him to take in. Both Pete and Ray reeled in their lines, and sat on the bank, since fishing was no longer the day's priority.

Ray then told Pete, "This device has several uses, one of them is that it is a telephone." "Do you mean that I can dial someone with this device and talk with them? I don't see any dial." Pete said.

"No, this is more like a radio telephone, you just push buttons." Ray answered as he was calling up the keyboard portion of his telephone.

"I don't see any buttons to push, just pictures of buttons, is that what you push?" Pete asked.

"Yes, that is what you push. The telephone portion of this device is not working right now because it needs to connect to a central location, what we call a network." Ray explained. "This device also connects you to all of the collected knowledge in the world, kind of like a mega library.

"The future must be amazing, full of highly educated people in the world using this device," Pete said.

"Um, not really," Ray answered back.

"This device allows instant communication around the world of voice, image, and ideas," said Ray.

"The future must have a new age of enlightenment," said Pete.

"Um, not really," said Ray.

"Are you telling me that this device has led to more and bloodier wars?" Pete asked. "No, not really," said Ray, "we still have religion and politics to create wars though."

"Then what do people do with this amazing device?" Pete asked.

"Well, we mostly use it to look at pictures of our pets and get into arguments with strangers." Ray answered. Ray then showed Pete a picture of his dog, "Molly".

"This device is so common that everyone carries one, even children." Ray said. "I guess that's why we do not use this device to its potential, it's just a common part of everyday life."

"How many years in the future are you from?" Pete asked.

"A little over 65 years," Ray answered.

"It's hard to believe that technology has grown so much in such a little time, we just got dial telephones a couple years ago," Pete said.

"I brought this device here to show it to you, to prove that I am from the future. I will not be born for another 15 years, and then in the year 1988, I will graduate from high school. My friend Martin and I need a lawyer to put together a trust fund for us, that we may collect upon our high school graduation. My friend, Martin Miles will have a list of companies to invest in at certain times, it will be up to you to make the investments for us. If you would like to get rich too, I suggest that you make those same investments. I will introduce you to Martin Miles tonight, who will give you specific instructions on what to invest, and when to invest it. Martin is also from the future. Do you think we have a deal?"

Pete's head was still spinning from all the information that Ray gave him, but he still had enough sense to say, "Yes, we have a deal."

"As a show of good faith, and if you promise to never show this device to anyone, I will give you this device," Ray said.

"It does not have any of the communication or library features, it will only function as a camera for you, and you will not be able to print out the pictures. At least for another 60 years.

This device has a very flat built-in battery. Tonight, when you meet Martin, I will give you the battery charger. The internal battery in this device needs to be charged daily, you simply plug the charger into the wall, and set the phone on top of it. This device should remain live for about another year, and then you will no longer be able to charge up the battery. I suggest that you play with it and learn everything that is inside of it." Ray said.

"Also, I must warn you. There are also some games in this device to play, they are great time wasters.

Ray then showed Pete how to take pictures with the cell phone, and also how to do a video. Pete was like a kid on Christmas morning, he was photographing everything he saw at the river. Ray also showed Pete how to delete images. And Ray suggested to Pete that he shouldn't delete the images that he took, as they were a look into the future.

While Pete was photographing everything in sight, Ray casted out into the river, and began fishing again. It only took Ray a couple hours to limit out for the day, with a couple coho salmon.

Ray had Pete follow him to the cafe, where he introduced Marty to Pete. Ray told Marty that Pete was brought up to date on their situation, and that he would help them.

However, Pete did look at Marty like he was from another planet. It did not phase Marty at all, he realized that Pete was most likely in shock with all the information he heard that day. Marty said that he would be home around 6:00, and the two guys should be ready with all the information that Pete was going to bring forward. The three salmon caught that day were left at the cafe for tomorrow's special-salmon steaks!

CHAPTER TWELVE

"Rocket 88"

Marty arrived home a little after 6:00, went to his house, picked up some paperwork, and went next door to see Pete and Ray playing games with the cell phone at Ray's place. Marty explained to Pete what needed to be done. He also brought out a series of envelopes with years on them. Marty gave Pete specific instructions only to open the envelope for the year that it currently was, because it could mess with the timeline, and any future investments might not prove fruitful. He also gave instructions about the Rolex watches. Since neither Ray nor Martin had been born yet he gave Pete instructions as to where and when they would be born, and where they would live. Ray and Marty each gave Pete one of their business cards, to make sure that he got the spelling of their names correct. They also gave a warning to Pete that he should probably only invest locally after he made his profits in the stock market. The idea being that the smaller the circle of influence, the less chance he had of messing up the timeline. Marty also explained that he was planning to remain in 1955 for an undetermined length of time, while Ray was currently trying to return to the present day.

After a long evening of conversation, Pete left with the cell phone, a cell phone charger, and an armload of papers to study.

In addition to all the paperwork that Marty had brought to Ray's house, were the three copies of "Rocket 88" that had showed up that day. Now it was just a matter of Sears delivering the turntable and Marty wiring it up to his ham radio. Marty and Ray stayed up talking about Pete, and if they thought he would do what was requested. They both decided that he was a pretty good choice.

Even though they did not have the record turntable yet, in a few hours Marty was still going to attempt more bridge crossings. He truly was a stubborn Finn, who would never give up.

After a few hours of sleep, Ray got into his car and headed for the bridge. It was a beautiful morning, and the steam/fog was rising off the North River. But it was another morning of futility, so Ray headed into work. He was thinking that if the song didn't trigger a reverse time slip, it would be time for him to start writing. He bought that typewriter after all.

Despite only having a few hours sleep, Pete went to the gas station to talk with Ray. He asked Ray if he could talk with him and Marty tonight also. Ray said, "Absolutely, the more you know, the better it will be for all of us."

Pete thanked Ray for including him in this opportunity to work with someone from the future, and the chance to be rich. Even though there was no element of chance to it, because the financial outcome was known. At least by Ray and Marty.

Pete made a point that evening, that he was actually taking a chance on these two time travelers as much as they were taking a chance on him. Marty reassured him that he would find out for himself, once the first round of investing paid off.

The first envelope was opened that evening, the stock was selected, the beginning value was listed, and the value at the end of the investment period was also listed. It was a company that Pete had never heard of, so it would be a leap of faith to invest in it. This would be a pattern that Pete would need to follow through all of the investments. Marty was glad to have a young person with an open frame of mind, to do these investments.

Many details were discussed that evening, Marty had the brain for finance, so Ray just stood back and let him, and Pete talk everything out.

The box from Sears showed up that day with the record turntable in it, now it was just a matter of Marty wiring it up to his modified ham radio transmitter. There would not be any work on the transmitter and turntable that evening because two late nights of discussing financial details totally wore Marty out.

Marty and Ray agreed that they would attempt the bridge crossing with the ham radio on the first day of good weather. The long-range weather forecast predicted cloudy skies every day of the week, clearing up on Saturday, which would now be their first chance.

That the weather was bad, was okay with the guys because it was imperative that Ray received another paycheck at least in the $400 to $500 range to be able to make investments. Ray worked that week at Fred's Super Shell Service doing everything he could to get the largest paycheck possible.

Every evening the guys would test out the radio to see if it would transmit to Ray's car. And every evening the radio transmissions got better. Ray was so ready to go home that he had his car packed Thursday night.

Friday was a hectic day for Ray, he got off early so he could cash his paycheck and give the money to Marty. He would not be needing any of it if he went home. Marty gave Ray his cell phone. He put a video on it telling the world that he was okay, it's just that he would not be back for the foreseeable future. He is on a sabbatical. He also had Ray take several pictures of him and Rita with Ray's Kodak brownie camera.

Marty left a long list of instructions on paper for his brother, instructing him to take over the company, and specifically to not sell the company.

Saturday morning rolled around, the weather was perfect, Marty had prepared a checklist of things that he needed to do. He turned on the transmitter, and gave it plenty of time to warm up, as it was a tube radio. He made sure all the connections between the turntable and the radio were secure, and gave Ray a thumbs up, it was time for him to take off for the bridge. Ray was more than ready, he had his car radio on full blast, already tuned to the frequency that they were transmitting on. Ray staged himself right in front of the bridge, the piano intro came on and he slowly drove onto the fog/steam covered bridge. He stopped in the middle of the bridge, and when the lyrics "Goin' 'round the corner" started, that was all that was needed because- "BAWHOOM!" happened, just like before, and the car died.

The car coasted to the other side of the bridge, just like before. Only this time he was going the opposite direction. Ray crossed his fingers that the car would start. And due to Ray's wisdom of buying a new battery, it turned over and started right up. Now the big question. Where or when was he? The first thing Ray did however, was look at his reflection in the rear view mirror.

CHAPTER THIRTEEN

"I've got something to tell you..."

Marty continued to transmit for around 10 minutes, then he shut it off. He figured that would be plenty enough transmission to get Ray across the bridge.

Marty got into the cafe's pickup truck and drove to the bridge. There was no sign of Ray, so Marty figured that he made it. Hopefully, he didn't age 65 years during the reverse time slip.

A feeling of loneliness crept over Marty, now that Ray had gone back to the present time. Sure, there was Rita, and he certainly could spend the rest of his life with her. However, there was no shared experience of living in two different timelines.

Marty decided that he needed to come clean with Rita. He needed to let her know that he was from the future, if they were to have a future together. He also decided that he was going to ask Rita to marry him, once he told her the truth.

Marty got to the cafe around 8:15, and the breakfast rush was very much underway.

Rita greeted Marty with the news that his car title had arrived, and he could now license his car. Things were coming together for Marty in 1955.

Marty told Rita that Ray had called his mother and found out she was in the hospital, and that Ray decided to move back to the Seattle area. He also called Fred at the service station and told him the same story, and that Ray would most likely not be back.

Marty was very nervous; Rita meant a lot to him and he wanted to make sure that the talk went well that evening. He figured that since his laptop was in the trunk of his car that he would show it to her, that night, after the cafe closed. In between taking orders from customers, Marty stopped Rita for a moment and said "I have something to talk about tonight. Let's hang around here at the cafe after we close."

Rita said, "Sure babe, we can make ourselves a nice romantic dinner here."

They closed the cafe a little early that night. They had not had a lot of time together since Ray came into town.

They set up a table in the back of the cafe so anyone looking in wouldn't see them. Marty grabbed both of Rita's hands and said, "Babe, I've got something to tell you. We have been together for a little over a year now, and I feel that you need to know this."

"Yes," said Rita with anticipation.

"I am from the future," said Marty.

"What?" Rita asked. "I thought you were going to propose to me. What are you talking about?"

Marty reached down for the box with the laptop in it, pulled it out and set it on the table. "This device is a computer from the future, I need to explain my situation to you. And yes, I'm asking you to marry me, but not before you know my entire story."

"You're not kidding, you need to explain yourself to me," Rita said. "I never expected a proposal to start with 'I'm from the future'." The first question I have, said Rita is, "Are you from planet Earth, and are you a human being?"

Marty said, "I am from Seattle, and I am a human being, and I am definitely in love with you,"

"Tell me about this thing," Rita said as she turned the computer around so it was facing her.

Marty answered, "I own a company that makes programs for these computers. They help the user do many things with this computer. I am from approximately 65 years in the future. I truly do not know why I am here in this period in time. Maybe it is to meet you. My car went through something called a time slip, and I ended up here. You were kind enough to help me and get me on my feet. I cannot possibly tell you how much you mean to me. You took me in and helped me. I'm sure that you have many questions about my past but have been kind enough not to ask them. I think that I may be able to return to where I came from, but I would like to stay with you. My business in the future is thriving, I am currently worth 1.2 billion dollars there. Yet, I would give that up to stay with you here."

"1.2 billion dollars? Either the money is worthless, or you are an idiot." Rita said.

"The money is not worthless, in fact it's quite a bit of money, but I love you and I would love to spend the rest of my life with you." Marty said. "I have had many girlfriends in the future, but I was never sure if they loved me, or my money. You, however, have shown me love when I had nothing. You trusted me and took me in to be your partner in this cafe. I hope that I have lived up to everything you were looking for in a person."

"That, you have been," said Rita. "Now tell me about this thing you call a computer, what does it do?"

"Well, you can use it for many things, you can keep a company's books on it, you can do scientific research with it, you can listen to music on it, it can be a library for you, I have several informational books on finance from 1955 to the Future on it. We can invest in companies that we know will do well, and withdraw investments before they go bad."

"You're telling me that you know how to make profitable investments, and we may never have to work here," Rita said.

"Absolutely," said Marty.

"But you already have 1.2 billion dollars in the future?" Rita asked.

"That, I do," said Marty.

"Then it really doesn't matter where or when you are, you will be rich," Rita said. "I think I could put up with that, so the answer is Yes, I will marry you."

Rita said, "I have a confession to make, when I first met you, I saw that you had a Rolex on your wrist. When you took it off to help me with the dishes, I could tell by the suntan on your wrist that it had been there a long time. I knew you were not a destitute person."

"But you still trusted me, and never questioned me," Marty said. "I feel that I owe you so much, because of that."

Marty then showed Rita pictures of his corporate headquarters and of his mansion, on the computer.

Rita asked Marty, "If we went to your time, would you still have to work, or could we travel and enjoy life."

"I have a brother that could run the company, I hope he has done well in my absence. That would be the big issue if we went to my time," Marty said.

"It seems that regardless of where we are, that we will be working, whether it's here at the cafe or at your business in the future," said Rita. "It sure would be nice to retire early and travel. How long do you think your investments here will take to pay off?"

"It will probably take about 10 years here, before we could retire from the cafe," said Marty. "But I promised Ray that I would stay in Grays Harbor county, because I did not want to prevent his birth."

Marty then explained to Rita how he thought the time slip happened, and that's how Ray showed up. He's also said that he was pretty sure that Ray went back to his timeline, and that they would most likely never see him again. Unless they went forward in time. He also explained that he did not know whether they would age 65 years if they also crossed over the bridge. If they made that decision, it would have to be a joint decision between the two of them.

CHAPTER FOURTEEN

"Epilogue"

Ray was relieved when he looked in the mirror and he had not aged. Now, where or when was he? It didn't take too long before he saw one of those new GMC pickups with the LED headlights towing a car on a trailer. As the truck got closer he read the writing on the door, it said "Johnson Property Management". He was home, finally after a tough few weeks. Then he noticed a Subaru WRX on the trailer, it said "M. Johnson Driver" on the door. It totally caught him off guard, he realized it was Mary, and she was heading out for either some practice runs or driving in a rally. He mashed on the brakes, at the same time, so did the GMC pickup. Mary recognized his car from the car show.

The first thing Mary said was "I missed you during the practice day, were you selling the Buick?"

To which Ray replied, "I'm sorry, I can't really explain what happened. The past couple weeks have been a blur. I am so glad to see you."

Which was very true, because Ray was glad to see anyone from the present day. Ray ran up to Mary and gave her a big hug, this caught Mary a little bit off guard because she was thinking he had been stand-offish to her.

"The truth is," Ray said, "I have been missing you, and I am so glad to see you. Are you going to the rally, or is this another practice session?"

Rita answered back, "The race is next Sunday, I figured I would get out the Subie, and run it through its paces. And to stop at the Brooklyn tavern too. Would you like to join me?"

"Actually, I would like that a lot. If you don't mind though, I would like to ride in your truck, I'm not really so hot about driving my Ford across that bridge again." Ray said.

"Oh, did you get caught in a time slip on your last trip across it?" Mary said very nonchalantly.

"Time slip? Don't know what you're talking about." Ray said nervously.

Mary reached for her wallet in her purse, and pulled out two very old business cards, one was Ray's, the other was Marty's. They were the ones that the guys had given Pete back in 1955.

Ray's jaw dropped open in astonishment. He said "Where did you get those?"

Mary answered, "My father was a lawyer by the name of Pete Johnson, he told me the story of two men trapped in a time slip in 1955. These two men told him what to invest in, in the stock market. He became very rich because of it, and he bought several properties in the Aberdeen area. You see, if it wasn't for you, I wouldn't have everything that I have now. You made me a very rich person. I just needed to meet you and Martin. For the longest time, I did not believe the story my father had told me until Martin disappeared a year ago. I went to your shop and had you build a car for me, and obviously you knew nothing about what happened to Martin. I figured at some point that you would also fall into the time slip. I have been hoping to join you in that time slip. Because I only knew my father as an old man, he married a younger woman, my mother, and I was born in 1980. Is Martin here with you?"

Ray was absolutely flabbergasted about the knowledge that this is Pete's daughter, and she knows about the time slip. He answered Mary's question with "No, he's not here, he decided to stay in 1955. Do you know if he returns to the present day?"

"No, that would be the future, and I do not know the future." Mary answered.

Ray parked the Ford, and then got into Mary's truck. It was nice to sit in a modern vehicle again, Ray didn't think he ever would. Ray also got a chance to meet Mary's dog "Kissa", and it reminded him how much he missed his dog, "Molly".

When the truck got to the bridge, Ray closed his eyes as he was afraid of another time slip. Nothing happened, and that made him a very happy person. He got his first glimpse of North River Road in the present day. The newspaper boxes that were attached to mailboxes were made of plastic and square, and the Burma shave signs were gone. When he got to where Uno lived there was just a Prius in the driveway, No signs of model T's anywhere. Mary pulled the truck and trailer into the parking lot of the Brooklyn tavern. He looked for Rita's Place, and saw where it should be. It was now an empty parking lot. He wondered what had happened, did the place burn down and just never get rebuilt, or have Marty and Rita gone to the present day and he just hasn't seen them yet. After all, he stopped when he recognized Mary right after he crossed the bridge.

The very first thing that Ray did when he got to the tavern, was excuse himself to go to a telephone and call his mother.

He told his mother that he was okay, and he would explain things when he got home later that day. Right now, he was visiting with a friend and after lunch, he was going to hit the road. He had his mother put "Molly" on the phone. She got very excited the second she heard Ray's voice, and she started barking. She was scolding him for taking off again. It was the best scolding that Ray had ever heard in his life. He promised her they would never be separated again. When he hung up from his mother, he called his shop only to find that things had been running very smoothly. The buyer for Invictus had been calling to shop daily to see if Ray was there though. He told his shop foreman Diego to give the buyer a call and tell him that he would be there Monday morning. He also told Diego to tell the guys at the shop that they really didn't need to work Saturday, and to take the rest of the day off- paid.

Mary and Ray had lunch and a couple of beers each. Mary explained that she wanted to meet Ray and Marty for quite a long time, and with Marty disappearing she realized that now was the time to act. She was as confused as the guys were. She told Ray that she knew that he would be at Rod Run, and to contact him before he also disappeared. She also knew that she would sound like a crazy lady if she mentioned the entire time slip thing to him, so she did her best to become friends with Ray.

As much as Mary wanted to continue talking with Ray, he said that he needed to get back to Federal Way to see his mother and pick up "Molly".

Much to Mary's surprise, Ray hugged Mary, and gave her a kiss on the cheek. He said he would be in touch with her this week and would love to be on her race team next Sunday.

Mary drove Ray back to the Ford, and they parted ways, for now. Ray was glad to get back to Highway 101. He drove up to Artic where Fred's Super Shell Service was, and you could never even tell there was a gas station there. He spent an amazing couple weeks with Fred, who is a wonderful boss. He hoped that Fred continued on with everything that he had started for him. Perhaps he can Google Fred and find out. The rest of the drive to his mother's house went without incident. He was even happy to see the usual Saturday afternoon traffic jam in Tacoma on the way home.

He got to his mother's house late in the afternoon. The moment that "Molly" saw him, she started jumping up and down. He was grateful to hug his mother, this was the best homecoming he has ever had.

Ray spent the next couple hours trying to explain everything to his mother. He showed her Marty's telephone and the message to his brother. Plus, he had his typewriter, his brownie camera, the car show stuff, and his fishing gear in the trunk of the Ford. He also showed his mother the suntan line on his wrist where his Rolex was. She was slowly becoming a believer of this incredibly tall tale, and very glad he was home, and not someplace else like Marty.

Ray and "Molly" went home that evening. It was the best feeling that he could possibly have, to sleep in his own bed.

He woke up several times during the night wondering if it all had been a dream, but it had not been. He got up in the morning, and for the first time in a few weeks, he and "Molly" went for a walk. Even though it was Sunday, he decided that he wanted to go to the shop and see how projects are progressing. He was quite impressed by the work that Diego had done in his absence. The idea of retirement crossed his mind once again. Molly went to her bed in his office and took a nap. He was thinking that was a pretty good idea, he sat in his office chair and dozed at his desk, when his phone rang.

It was a female voice at the other end of the line, it said 'Dah-Di-Dah-Dit Dah-Dah-Di-Dah'," he recognized the voice, it was Rita! That meant that Marty and Rita figured out how to make it back to the present day.

This took so much pressure off Ray. He was not going to have to explain anything to Marty's brother, he made it home. And it also meant, no more monthly visits from the FBI.

Rita put Marty on the phone, and he said "It was a wise move to buy an automatic turntable, we just set the record to play over and over again, as far as I know it's still playing in 1955. Rita and I decided that we wanted to take a chance and come back here,

I am glad you made it safely here. We called your house, and got no answer, so I figured I would give the shop a try. It was such a relief when you picked up. We had no problems with aging, I assume the same for you."

"Made it here safely with no aging problems whatsoever," Ray answered." "And, I managed to see Mary when I came across the bridge, I am going to the rally race with her team next Sunday,"

Marty called his brother to let him know that he was home and that he would be in the office on Monday. And that he had someone for his brother to meet, a very special person in his life.

Ray finished the transaction to sell Invictus on Monday morning, and it went to its new home that day. He attended the board of directors meeting of Marty's company that afternoon with "Molly" on his lap. Things were back to the way they should be, and now "Molly" would travel everywhere with Ray. She now had her own seat belt that she wore in whatever rig she was riding in. She was not going to be left behind ever again.

Ray met up with Mary that week, and he became a member of her team's pit crew. She took second place in the rally that Sunday. They celebrated at the Brooklyn tavern. At the end of the evening, Mary suggested to Ray that he put a trailer hitch on the back of the Ford and procure a solid state transmitter that he could wire directly to the Ford's AM radio. She then said, "Let's go get some model T's."....

Made in the USA
Las Vegas, NV
06 March 2023

68608018R00080